Aftermath

Buried Secrets, Hidden Truths, Missing Chapters

Book Five of the Destined Series

Michael D Brooks

Cover art includes Public Domain images from Canva, AI created images using the Canva app Magic Media, and images created by the author. Cover design by Michael D Brooks.

Independently Published, May, 2026

Author's Note:
This book was written entirely by me. I used generative AI tools to help refine the prose, tighten passages, and occasionally expand on ideas I had already developed. All story elements, characters, and creative direction are my own.

ISBN: 979-8-9877448-4-0
ISBN: eBook 979-8-9877448-5-7

Contents

Acknowledgements

My Beta Readers:
Projekt_itachi
Linda Stokes
Gregory Stubblefield

The usual band of suspects.

The many readers who have taken the time to follow, rate, review, and support.

Thank you.

Chapter 1

A warm breeze whipped across the rocky precipice of Lookout Cove and softly whistled through its outcroppings as Progensha's two suns slowly set below the mountain range dividing the horizon. Each yellow ball of light contributed to the sky's peach hue which glowed behind a thin blanket of white clouds in an otherwise orange evening sky. The cove was an observation post tucked neatly into a deep crevice carved along an upper ridge of the Mountain of the Goddess by ancient winds.

A small, diverse group of onlookers stood along its edge. A gray stone wall railing was the only barrier that kept someone from accidentally falling to the ground below. The motley collection of individuals stared out at the desolate valley in the distance far below. Among those individuals was Zuri Lin-Piper. She was an unassuming young woman of Terran ancestry whose physical stature did not come anywhere near the rough nature of her personality. Her olive skin tone contrasted sharply with the mop of bright ginger-colored hair that flapped in the wind. It framed a round, youthful face accented with slender brown eyes, high cheekbones, a pug nose, and lots of tiny tan freckles. She liked to say she got the best and worst qualities of her parents.

Zuri surveyed the land through a pair of magnifiers and tears. Her feelings were a swirling mixture of sadness, loss, regret, and rage that laid heavy on her heart. A black cape she wore draped over her samurai-style military uniform snapped like a flag in the wind. What she could see appeared inhospitable, dank, and foreboding. It was a grotesque reminder of what the land looked like sols earlier when a bustling city, thriving villages, abundant food fields, livestock, thick forests, and lush hills teeming with life had existed. Now it was all a veritable wasteland.

The devastation stretched to the horizon and beyond the limits of the best magnifiers. The remnants of what were once buildings lay in small, unrecognizable crumpled heaps. Girders were now the size of small tree branches, broken bits of concrete slabs could fit in the palm of a hand, and glass fragments resembled tiny bits of micro crystal. They were all that remained of a sprawling city and the surrounding valley.

Traveler City was once a flourishing urban center, but now it was just a memory. Wiped from existence in an instant by an unprecedented explosion. Every fabricated physical object within the destruction radius was gone. Every biological lifeform was reduced to its smallest molecular particle. What had been a luscious green landscape, abundant with life, was reduced to an endless patch of crumbling gray grit.

The area looked like a featureless moonscape. Not even the clouds in the sky directly over the barren ground escaped the carnage. The normally fluffy white mists of water vapor hung in an orange sky like tattered gray rags. They obscured direct sunlight from the planet's two suns. Light rain fell from them, permeated the ground, and soaked whatever remained. The clouds outside of the destruction zone hung in the sky in their normal configurations of floating, pillows of moist mist.

It's as if the Goddess herself is crying from the heavens, Zuri thought.

She lowered the magnifiers and let them dangle around her neck as her eyes shimmered with tears. Zuri mourned for everything and everyone lost. But the greatest pain she felt was for her parents, Memphis Lin and Nicholas Piper.

Her great-grandmother, Martina, told her they perished in a final desperate effort to save the survivors and refugees of a protracted war, and destroy sensitive information. What Martina did not tell her was the true reason her parents died. They were victims of a weapon from the future; from another universe.

Only four people knew of the weapon's existence and now two of them were dead. What they did not know at the time was its full destructive potential. The resulting carnage was unexpected and unprecedented. No one on the planet had ever witnessed anything like it. In the blink of an eye a significant portion of a continent was wiped from existence.

Why? Why did this have to happen? Why do we get to live and they don't? Zuri wondered.

The city-state of Uderra survived mostly unscathed from the brunt of the destruction. The Uderrans, who once called part of the devastated area home, were located far enough away from the epicenter and blast radius to be spared. An extensive mountain range and a few inland seas helped shield them.

Displaced years before by a ruthless enemy, the former Plains People, led by Zuri's parents, fled to a virgin territory of land surrounded by verdant hills, crystal waters, tall mountains, and a fecund vale. They called the territory Uderra, which meant reborn in the language of the Plains People, and rebranded themselves Uderrans. Together with other war refugees, they cultivated the land and transformed it into their new home.

As a child, Zuri had spent her formative years in Traveler City, but when the Plains People relocated, she grew up in Uderra and followed in her parents' footsteps and became an officer in the Uderran military. She sniffled as she thought of all the people who were not so fortunate.

As she surveyed the land, it appeared to her only inorganic geologic matter as well as water were spared. The mountains and seas escaped the carnage. She lowered herself to the ground and sat in sorrowful silence and tried to make sense of it all.

The planet would be forever changed by the insane power of a weapon that should have never existed. As Zuri grieved, she wondered what could have been done differently.

The official story was that her parents stayed behind to destroy sensitive information that had not yet been transferred from Martina's home to the royal vault in Uderra, and to assist with the evacuation of stragglers. They planned to rendezvous with others once the data was destroyed, but they never made it. Martina said her parents sacrificed themselves to save their world. Which was not far from the truth, but from where she sat, much of the world looked like it had ended. As far as she was concerned, the one she knew certainly had.

Zuri mourned her loss as her great-grandmother, father-in-law, and a few curious onlookers accompanied her. They all tried to make sense of what they witnessed. Each in their own way. Overwhelmed by grief, she lowered her head, buried her face in her great-grandmother's bosom and wept.

"Why? Why did it have to end this way, Gran?" she sobbed.

Her great-grandmother sat on the ground with her and held her tight. Martina, a woman whose gray complexion and feline facial features framed two pools of jet black eyes with no visible irises, indicative of her Selemite and Felidian heritage, breathed deeply as her silvery hair fluttered in the strong breeze.

We were out of options, is what she thought. What she said was, "Your parents were the unfortunate victims of an unfathomable act." She gazed out toward the desolation, sighed and thought, *It should have been me. It was supposed to be me.*

Zuri sensed the older woman's abject anguish and stared directly into Martina's eyes and said, "It's not fair."

The older woman held her great-granddaughter's look and said, "Many times in our lives life does not seem fair, my child." She paused and looked out over the valley, then sighed before she continued, "If it is any consolation, they are with the Goddess now."

"Why couldn't the Goddess let them live full lives before she took them?"

"That is not for us to know," Martina said.

"The Goddess can go to the Underworld for all I care," Zuri said.

Martina stroked her great-granddaughter's hair and said, "You don't really mean that."

"Yes, I do." The anger in her tone was palpable.

A deep voice emanated from a clean-shaven man with dark brown skin and light green eyes who stood next to them. He said, "Lady Martina, Lady Zuri, let us return home and soothe our sorrows in the comfort of our homes amongst our families and friends. We shall plan our future course of action with the next dawn's light."

Martina looked up at her grandson-in-law with the pained expression of someone whose soul was tortured and said, "You are quite right, T'iang. Let us leave this place."

She reached for his outstretched hand and let him lift her from the ground and into her wheelchair. Looking over at her great-granddaughter, she asked, "Are you coming?"

"In a micton," Zuri said.

As the others left to return to their homes, Zuri continued to think of her parents. She looked up toward the sky and said, "I will make you proud. Your sacrifice will not have been in vain."

Chapter 2

A solitary figure stood on a rocky hill far from the destruction zone, but close enough to witness the results of the cataclysm that wiped a sizable portion of the planet's surface and population from existence. From his vantage point, Nadir saw the aftermath of the largest explosion ever witnessed on Progensha. Never in his wildest imaginings did he conceive such devastation possible. He wondered who could have engineered such a feat. He rubbed a calloused hand through a sandy mop of hair and pondered what he saw before him.

The splotch of lifelessness stretched to the horizon and beyond. He knew the actions of his people contributed to what happened. If they had simply left the Travelers, the Plains People, and the Wanderers alone, everything would be where it should have been. Nowhere in recorded or unrecorded history had there been anything like it. Could it have been the Travelers? The Uderrans? Someone or something else? The thought was unfathomable. He knew the unbridled hatred his people had for the Travelers and all those who were allied with them, and the war they waged against them led to the devastation he now witnessed.

Nadir had been taught from infancy that his people, the Thourons, were the Goddess's chosen, superior to all others by divine right. It was the natural order of things. He was indoctrinated in the belief to the point of religious fanaticism. At one time, like so many others, he unquestionably adhered to the rhetorical doctrine instilled in all Thourons. But as he grew older, he questioned that belief system when he witnessed the oppression and persecution of those who dared to publicly question the status quo. A few people he called friends had simply disappeared never to be heard or seen again. Official reports placed the blame on the people of the valley. However, Nadir had his own theories about what might have happened to them.

It was the vicious and cruel treatment of non-Thourons that caused him to doubt the righteousness of their cause, and to question the benevolence of the Goddess herself. The actions of his people felt like a perversion of the Goddess's intentions. It was pure arrogance for them to say Her word applied to only Thourons and not to all Progenshans. As a child, he was taught that She is the Mother Creator. The Goddess to all Progenshans. They were all her children; she just loved some more than others. When he asked his teachers why would the Mother Creator not love all of Her children equally, he was emphatically told not to question the wisdom of the Goddess. But deep down in the pit of his soul, his doubts caused him to experience a spiritual epiphany. What if others were not inferior, just different?

Such thinking was considered disloyal, but as he began to question things that disturbed his soul, he wanted to know more. He needed to understand how things worked in the world. How everything was connected. But to question the status quo out loud meant to endure harsh criticism or worse. So he learned to conceal his insatiable curiosity and nurture his rebellious nature. He needed to find others who felt as he did without vanishing as so many others had. He joined the military and became an intelligence operative so that he could get closer to ascertaining information he believed would help him find answers to his many questions. But all he found were lies, twisted truths, subterfuge, and moral ambiguity. He had searched for a sense of righteous indignation, but had not found it. Nadir operated in a profession where shadow and light produced varying shades of gray.

He sat down on a small boulder and looked at his hands. They were pale like the rest of him, but not immune to getting dirty. Nadir knew he would need to eventually stop playing it safe. He would have to take some initiative and be a catalyst of change for the better. He wondered if he was willing to die trying. And if it came to that, would his death be a spark for positive change or be a brief, dying ember of no significance?

He had heard rumors of an underground resistance dedicated to undermining the abhorrent practices of a regime that professed to be civilized while perpetrating acts of barbarism towards others. He decided to seek out this underground. He would decide for himself where his ethical loyalties were. But how was he supposed to do that without being perceived as disloyal or a spy?

Though he considered himself a good judge of people, Nadir knew that the slightest misstep would be fatal. He did not wish to die before his death would have meaning. He was an intelligence officer, not a spy. He would need to bide his time, learn all that he could, hone his observation skills, and wait until he deemed the time was right for him to make his move. But for the moment, he needed to get back to his unit and report on what he learned from his scouting mission.

Nadir was lost in his thoughts when he heard movement behind him. He pulled out his sidearm, sprang off the boulder, pivoted toward the sound, and pointed his firearm at two of his comrades. He came close to discharging his pistol before he eased the pressure on his trigger finger.

“By the grace of the Goddess, you two were sectons away from becoming denizens of the ancestral realm,” he said, with a mixture of stress and relief in his voice. “What are you doing here?” After a moment’s hesitation, he holstered his weapon.

His two closest friends stood before him in their dingy brown military uniforms, hands raised, frozen in place with looks of astonishment and uncertainty on their pale faces. As the shock and fear of nearly being killed wore off, their light pastel pink complexions slowly returned.

Naron, who was a head taller and stockier than Nadir, was the first to recover from his shock before he spoke. He ran a beefy hand with sausage-like fingers through his thick mane of blonde hair.

"You have been gone for more than ten sols," he said. "We grew concerned."

He looked at his companion, Andorra, for assurance.

With what sounded like sincere concern, she said, "Yes, we thought maybe you might have fallen victim to whatever befell this place." She gestured with a sweeping motion of her arm toward the desolation in the distance.

Andorra was the same height as Nadir, and just five cycles older than Nadir and Naron. But her face, once smooth and youthful in a doughy sort of way, was now gaunt displaying the weariness of someone who had seen more than her share of the worst war could offer, and the ugliest manifestations within people's hearts. For someone so young, her mostly black hair was heavily accented by copious strands of gray.

"Friends," Nadir began, "I have been gone for longer periods of time on scouting missions."

"But that was territory familiar to us," Naron said. "This ... this destruction laid an unknown at our feet. We did not and do not know what to expect. There has never been anything like this in the history of our people."

"Yes," Andorra said. "For all we knew, you were engulfed by whatever happened out there. We came to lend assistance, and to see for ourselves the aftermath."

Nadir was pensive for a moment before he replied. "I thank you for your concern." He turned to face the valley then said, "But as you can see, if something had happened to me, your assistance would have been in vain." He looked out at the desolation then back at Naron before he said, "A more accurate description would be to say, there has never been anything like this in the history of the planet."

A whipping wind passed through the moments of silence that signaled none of them knew what else to say before Andorra finally asked, “How could this happen?”

Naron snorted. “I think the better question to ask is how do we exact revenge?”

Chapter 3

As Progensha's waning suns slipped below the mountain peaks and seemed to reluctantly give way to the encroaching darkness, Zuri continued to sit on the ground thinking and plotting as she watched the bevy of shimmering points of light appear in the transitioning sky like apparitions. The Plains People called the night sky the Great Beyond. She studied those points of light and wondered what it would be like to travel among them as her parents had. They had referred to it as space. Her thoughts were interrupted by the sound of footsteps lightly crunching gravel approaching from behind. She slowly reached for the pistol at her side beneath her cape and analyzed the sound.

"That's far enough," she said with a menacing tone that matched the wind's chill.

The footsteps stopped and just the wind made a sound before a silky soft male voice asked, "Are you planning on harming the love of your life?"

She smiled and said, "Only if the love of my life is planning on doing something stupid." She relaxed the grip on her gun.

T'yree, Zuri's husband and the youngest son of T'iang, said, "Where you are concerned I may be inclined to do anything deemed stupid."

"Softly walking up behind a distraught warrior is indeed stupid. You are fortunate I know the sound of your footfalls."

"And that is why I was not concerned."

He sat on the ground next to his wife, wrapped a beefy arm around her shoulders, and pulled her close. She turned her head to look up at him. His deep chocolate brown skin and bald head, typical of both male and female Plains People, glistened in the receding sunlight. His emerald eyes appeared to twinkle against the waning light of the suns as they sank behind the darkening mountain peaks. Those lovely windows into his soul never failed to take her breath away whenever she gazed into them. He grinned at her with an alluring smile that was accompanied by the cutest dimple. She caressed his face with a hand and asked, "What did I do to ever deserve you?"

"Simply being born was enough."

She rested her head on his shoulder then winced and said, "Oh."

T'yree lightly touched her very pregnant belly and said, "The little one seems to be quite active this evening."

Zuri sighed and said, "That last kick was strong."

"Like his mother."

Zuri winced again. "Maybe too strong." She sighed and said, "I'm sorry my parents won't be here when our child is born."

"Although they are not with us, they are living in another plane of existence. They are with the Goddess now. I am sure they are looking down upon you."

Zuri thought it was interesting that her husband would use the term plane of existence. When her parents thought she was old enough to understand, they told her they had come to Progensha from somewhere in the depths of the Great Beyond. They made her promise never to reveal that she knew to anyone. Most Progenshans did not believe intelligent life existed beyond their world. If other people found out, it might cause trouble for them all. Martina and T'iang were the only people who knew the full truth. What they did not know was that Lin and Piper told their daughter where they came from. They had just never told her about *when* they came from. All Zuri knew was that her parents were from the Great Beyond. She did not know what the circumstances were that brought them to Progensha.

Another kick brought her back to the present.

"You think so?" she asked.

"I believe so."

She suspected that either Martina or T'iang had sent him to see how she was doing after her blasphemous outburst about the Goddess. Though she meant what she said at the time, she regretted saying it aloud.

"Lady Martina and my father told me what you said." His tone was even. There was not a hint of anger or disappointment in it.

Zuri sighed and said, "I figured one of them would have mentioned it."

"They are upset that you feel that way."

“How else am I supposed to feel?”

“Exactly as you do. But cursing the Goddess for something she did not do is ... harsh and unfair to the Mother Creator.”

She felt he was right. The Goddess gave them all free will, and what they did with it was their responsibility. But the choices they were sometimes forced to make could be excessive and extreme. She wondered what was a person supposed to do when the best decision they can make has dire consequences?

“Do you think She'll forgive me?”

“If you ask Her with a truly contrite heart.”

Though neither of her parents were particularly religious, Zuri felt she was at least a spiritual person. More or less. She silently asked the Goddess for forgiveness then asked T’yree, “So where do we go from here?”

He paused, looked out at the desolation as the shadow of night crept in to blanket it, heaved a heavy sigh then said, “We will have to see what others will do. The shock must run its course before people can move forward with their lives.”

“There are a lot of pieces that need to be picked up. I suppose gran will have ideas,” Zuri said.

“Of that I am certain. Lady Martina is always full of them.”

That isn’t all she’s full of, Zuri thought.

After a moment’s contemplation, T'yree said, “Following the new dawn, we shall commence discussing plans for the future. I am certain others will have varying ideas.”

“Of that I have no doubt,” Zuri said.

They were both alluding to the city’s council representatives. Their meetings were often raucous spectacles filled with political posturing and bluster. The council members tended to get in their own way and agreed to disagree in most instances. If it were not for the royal family having often to intervene, not much would have gotten accomplished.

"But for now," he continued, "We will enjoy what is left of the present. Let us get up from this uncomfortable ground and go home so we can soothe our sorrows in a more inviting environment."

Zuri let her husband help her stand then walked with him down the well-worn path back to the waiting chariot at the base of the mountain. T'yree helped his wife get into the passenger side and buckled her in, walked around the front of the vehicle, slid into the driver's seat next to her, and drove them back home to Uderra and an uncertain future.

Chapter 4

Palatial in size, the building Zuri and T'yree called home lacked any sign of opulence. The simplicity of its layout and the sparse decorations and furniture negated their status as members of the royal family. Its design matched that of the homes and businesses of the average citizen.

Before Uderra's founding, the royals lived amongst the common people; their social status was recognized and respected by the people as part of their customs. Living in close proximity to the average person served to instill a bond of trust and loyalty between them and their subjects. It was an arrangement that withstood the test of time for generations. They were not perceived as aloof, overbearing despots, but as caring, empathetic leaders who lived among the people, not above or apart from them.

Their culture, based on the teachings of the Goddess, was centered around a belief that all life was sacred, and that all people, regardless of their station in life, deserved to be treated with dignity. But when the conflict with the Thourons escalated, following a surprise attack resulting in the deaths of many residents of the valley, one of which included the queen's sister-in-law, and the loss of their ancestral home, those beliefs were put to the test. While a few questioned the validity of the Goddess's teachings, most continued to adhere to them. To ensure their cultural beliefs remained intact and that the Plains People could continue to live unharassed, they decided to relocate to Uderra.

In a rare break with tradition, it was decided by popular consensus that the royals should be protected from their enemies. So a structure was built that would serve as a fortress, a seat of government and power, and a refuge for the helpless. Based heavily upon the cultural influences of the Plains People, the structure reflected their modest tastes and practices. As a symbol of their commitment to protect their people, the royal family returned the favor and decreed that a physical wall be erected around the city.

The actual physical location and layout of the city were due in part to Zuri's parents, Martina, the royal family, and, in a small way, Zuri herself. As a testament to their cultural beliefs, they opened their new city to everyone fleeing from the tyranny of the Thourons. The Uderrans considered themselves blessed because their city was far enough away from the Thourons to provide them with a degree of isolation—if only for a short time.

Zuri's parents had discovered the location upon which Uderra was built. They persuaded T'iang and his sister, the queen, along with others, to join them. Martina was a key influencer in defining its boundaries, and also in furthering the expansion, construction, and fortifications of the city-state as it grew.

Though not a member of the Plains People, she was a respected elder in Traveler City before its tragic loss. Being related to the brother of the queen also helped. Zuri eventually joined the Uderran military when she came of age and became one of the head engineers.

Thanks to the ingenuity of the Traveler City engineers, the development of Uderra progressed rapidly. Much of the infrastructure of Traveler City was dismantled and transplanted. In just a few short cycles, Uderra rapidly grew and expanded into the Plains People's new seat of power.

Thouron aggression had not only displaced hundreds of Plains People and the many residents of Traveler City, but it also impacted the various pockets of towns, villages, and enclaves of people in the valley. Refugees seeking sanctuary brought their expertise in a multitude of trades, skills, and cultural influences with them. The development of the city was primarily driven by the Plains People and Traveler City residents. The forced amalgamation of disparate customs, beliefs, and philosophies, and an overwhelming need to defend themselves resulted in the birth of a burgeoning regional powerhouse. Its social, political, and economic influence continued to exponentially grow as more people emigrated to it.

The rapid expansion was not without its growing pains. The vastly disparate makeup of its citizenry sometimes resulted in contentious disagreements. Eventually, a government based on that of the Plains People, and a military patterned after the one Zuri's parents served in became the foundation upon which everything else was born. The Uderran mindset was fixated on becoming a formidable deterrent to the Thourons in as short a time as possible. The shared objectives were enough of a motivator to facilitate a need to swiftly resolve issues. The common denominator was the Thourons.

Since the focus was on defense, all dwellings were constructed with materials that would help them withstand conventional military weapons. Additionally, a concerted effort was placed on the development of sophisticated defensive weaponry of their own. The construction of the defensive wall around the city was accelerated. An underground complex was designed and constructed to house the military, medical, research, and fabrication centers. Bomb shelters and bunkers were built for the average citizen to seek refuge in until the perimeter fortifications could be completed. Every able-bodied individual from every trade worked long hours in shifts around the clock to get the job done.

Uderra's remote location and geographical features afforded it some protection from their enemy. The location and mountainous terrain without question protected the city when the rest of the continent was destroyed. Many believed the city was spared because it had openly accepted all the people the Thourons displaced in the war they waged against the residents of the valley. Some saw it as the Goddess bestowing her blessings upon them as the true inheritors of their world.

In the sols following the most devastating event in the planet's history, those who survived were evaluating their futures. A large majority were opting to leave Uderra and scatter to areas untouched by the blast or Thourons. They were motivated to move as far away from Thouron territory as possible. Martina was opposed to such measures and lobbied to persuade those who supported leaving to reconsider.

When Zuri and T'yree arrived back at their quarters, Martina wheeled herself from her suite and greeted them in the front room.

"I see your husband finally convinced you to come home," she said.

"It was not I who convinced her to return." T'yree pointed at his wife's belly.

"I see," Martina said. "Well, in that case, I suggest we all abide by the wishes of the head of this house."

Zuri was going to dispute Martina when she felt the baby kick. "Perhaps you're right, Gran."

"I know I'm right. Now let's get you off your feet. Grab my chair and roll me over to the recliner so you can sit."

Zuri used Martina's wheelchair as a walker and pushed her great-grandmother across the room and gingerly eased herself into the recliner. She kicked off her boots and rested her feet in a basin of warm water T'yree had run for her before he prepared the evening meal.

While Zuri rested and T'yree cooked, Martina wheeled herself around helping him. He learned early in his courtship to let Martina do whatever she wanted within reason. Which meant anything she wanted. Despite losing the use of her legs to a terrorist's bomb more than twenty cycles ago, the woman was fiercely independent and stubborn.

Once she made her mind up about something, a herd of wild ekwins could not get her to change it.

One of the rare times she relented was when Zuri's parents persuaded her to leave her home in Traveler City. Martina regretted her decision and blamed herself for their deaths. She kept herself busy to keep her mind off of what happened. Only she and T'iang knew the true reason for their sacrifice. And they were not talking.

T'yree put the finishing touches on their meal and brought Zuri and Martina their plates. Together they thanked the Goddess for their food, then T'yree fixed himself a plate and joined the ladies in the front room.

Chapter 5

They ate in reflective contemplation, mirroring the melancholy feelings everyone in Uderra felt. The dour mood was eventually broken when Zuri made a sound after the baby kicked. That is when Martina asked about the baby.

“When is the baby due? Any sol now?”

Zuri let out a gasp following another kick before she replied. “Yes, Gran. The healers said the baby could come at any time.”

“The nursery is ready. Are you?”

“More than you know.”

“Good. And since you’ve been granted extended bereavement and maternity leave, you’ll have adequate time to nurse and recuperate.”

“About that,” Zuri began, “I don’t see myself sitting around getting soft and becoming useless. I wish to stimulate my mind and rejuvenate my body while I am in convalescence. I would also like to dive through the archives you have amassed.”

Both curious and suspicious, Martina asked, “Why? You’ve never shown an interest in them before.”

“I’ve always been interested. I just never found the time to sit down and go over them. I have always been immersed in my duties. But now that I will have more time on my hands, when I am not tending to my daughter, I would like to make good use of it by reading the notes in the archives. Mother and father used to say they made for interesting reading. I also want to know my parents’ thoughts. They said they helped contribute to what you have amassed. And now that they are gone, I feel their loss and wish to be connected to them—even if it’s through the words they left behind. With my extended leave, I will finally have the time.”

Martina studied her great-granddaughter intently and was moved when Zuri’s eyes teared up. Knowing how much they both missed them, she gave the request a quick thought then said, “I will make them available for your use.”

“May I be included in this offer?” T’yree asked. “I have also been curious about the unspoken parts of our shared history.”

His query referred to the oral history of the Plains People and the recorded history of Traveler City. Very few people were privy to the full history of just how his people and the Travelers met. Of course there was the oral history, but the written history was something only a few were aware of. Not only was Martina the guardian of that written word, but she was also a descendant of the original Travelers. She was the last living person who knew some of her ancestors that settled in the valley before the Thourons began their war of aggression.

As a child, T'yree was taught that long ago a band of mysterious strangers appeared on the edge of the plains in desperate need of help from a major calamity that befell them. They were a motley group of strange looking people whose appearance and customs were unlike anything the Plains People had ever encountered. These strange travelers said their homes had been destroyed by a natural disaster and they were forced to flee their ancestral land. They said they came from a territory far beyond the known boundaries and had asked the Plains People for permission to resettle in the nearby glen.

Skeptical at first, his ancestors cautiously welcomed the strangers and helped them establish a community adjacent to the Great Plains near the Mountain of the Goddess and the Rocky Hills of the Thourons. Initially, the strangers isolated themselves for many cycles. Tyree's ancestors kept a wary eye on their new neighbors. Scouts reported seeing wondrous structures and vehicles. At first they thought the strangers were preparing to attack them. They proved to be industrious people. Their village rapidly grew into a town that continued to grow and expand. When it appeared to T'yree's ancestors the strangers did not intend to harm them, they cautiously approached and offered the hand of friendship.

In return, the newcomers, who called themselves Travelers, opened trade with the Plains People and other tribal groups. They shared their knowledge of agriculture, medicine, science, engineering, education, and other wondrous oddities. Over time, their settlement flourished and blossomed into a thriving city. Everyone lived in relative harmony until the Thourons decided those they deemed outsiders were a threat to their plans for regional dominance—particularly the Travelers.

For cycles, the Thourons had been more of a nuisance than a threat until they were unified under one banner and one cause. The recent destruction of the valley was the culmination of generations of violence against its inhabitants. And now people were asking if what happened a few sols ago was what happened to the original Travelers. The area beyond the borders of the nomadic tribes, from which the Travelers came, was now a dangerous wasteland occupied by monstrous beasts and a zone of radiation. It was known as the Land of No Return. If the key to discovering the truth to what precipitated it was in the archives that Lady Martina maintained, then finding that key was near the top of T'yree's to-do list–especially if his wife was considering something similar.

Martina stopped chewing and stared out into space. A veil of sadness appeared on her face before she replaced it with a smile and said, "It's nice to see young people taking an interest in learning about the past. Yes, I will make the archives available to you both. With all that has happened, I suppose it's the least I can do."

"Thank you, Gran."

"Yes, thank you, Lady Martina."

Martina scoffed. "Stop calling me that."

Zuri was content believing her great-grandmother did not suspect she had an ulterior motive. T'yree knew his wife well enough to know she was manipulating Martina. But neither suspected Martina was also devising a scheme of her own for her archives.

Chapter 6

The next sol, Zuri's plans were put on hold. She was in the Palace's main healing center screaming and cursing her husband and the healing staff as she gave birth to their child.

Very much like her mother, she swore every expletive that came to her mind in Uderran, Alliance Standard, Mandarin, and a few dialects neither T'yree nor Martina thought she knew. The two of them sat in a hallway outside the birthing room. T'yree cringed and squirmed in his chair as each curse echoed through the normally quiet halls. Martina, on the other hand, relaxed and composed, thought about the birth of her own daughter, Mar'jan, many cycles ago. The circumstances were nearly similar.

She remembered how she had called her mate every insulting vocabulary word that came to mind as he sat outside her birthing room. Her daughter's birth was not an easy one, and she did not have the benefit of either of her parents being present. Her mother died of natural causes when she was still a child, and her father went missing after a Thouron raid on a research facility shortly after she had come of age. So she had heaped all of her pain and loss on her partner. And he had accepted it with grace and understanding.

Things were good in the beginning. Though she and her partner never officially sanctified their union, they lived as if they had. On the eve of their daughter's Age of Maturity ceremony, Martina's beloved collapsed and fell unconscious. He died of congenital heart failure the next sol. His death devastated her. Mar'jan said she had become a crosspatch as a result. Of course she disagreed with her daughter's assessment.

Martina's trip down memory lane was interrupted when the sound of a baby crying replaced the cursing. The joyful sound reminded her of Mar'jan's first cries. Despite the struggles of raising a child as a single parent, her daughter grew up to become a respected healer and worked among the Plains People until her tragic death. She missed her dearly. The sol she received word of her daughter's death remained fresh in her mind. It had been many long cycles later, but Martina remembered it as if it was the sols before.

Mar'jan and her husband were killed when a medical facility they worked at in the Grassy Plains was attacked by a roving Thouron patrol. Martina was left to take care of her granddaughters, Jaydeen, Mona, and Sylvia. Forced into single-parent mode once again, she raised her granddaughters in modest surroundings in her quaint home in a quiet neighborhood in Traveler City.

Jaydeen and Mona were a few cycles older than Sylvia. When they came of age, they married successful merchants from the Grassy Plains.

Sylvia, Mar'jan's youngest, was a precocious child and displayed a talent for learning languages at an early age. By the time she came of age she spoke a variety of them. Her skill eventually led to a job as a translator at the Traveler City Cultural Exchange and Engagement Center. While on a much deserved break from work, she went to the Grassy Plains to visit her sisters, where she caught the eye of T'iang. He was the brother to the queen of the Plains People and well respected by everyone in the region. He had a reputation for being tough but fair, empathetic and compassionate. Wise beyond his years.

Initially, Sylvia did not believe she was worthy of the attention of a member of the royal family, but T'iang persisted in winning her affections. She eventually relented and allowed him into her life. They proved to be the perfect match for each other, and were married following a brief courtship.

Sylvia left her job and went to live with T'iang, but would often shuttle between Traveler City and the Grassy Plains to help her grandmother. Sometimes she would stay at Martina's home for sols just so her grandmother would have some company. T'iang offered Martina a place to live with the royals, but she always refused. She said she did not want to be a burden, and that it would take her away from her archives. She was well respected and liked by her neighbors. So they all looked out for her wellbeing. She repaid them by baking and cooking delectable meals and desserts, and babysitting their children.

Her house was a virtual repository of historical data stuffed full of cabinets, computers, storage devices, and miscellaneous material. So Sylvia would humor her grandmother and help her record, organize, and catalog her work.

It was during one of those visits that T'iang sent word that a hunting party found two strangely dressed people who were injured, malnourished, and near death following a dart lizard attack. Had the hunters not been tracking the lizard, the couple would have surely died from the lizard poison and been devoured by their predator. They were so close to death, it was decided they would not survive the trip to Traveler City. T'iang requested healers come to the Plains to attend to the medical needs of the couple.

With the help of the healers from Traveler City, the couple's injuries were tended to. T'iang also noted that following their recovery, the strangers spoke like Travelers, and asked peculiar questions about people and places unfamiliar to him or any of his people. T'iang thought Martina would be interested in meeting them. He said their names were Memphis Lin and Nicholas Piper, and that they came from somewhere called the Alliance. Martina was immediately interested in meeting them and asked that they be brought to her when they were well enough to travel.

Normally, such a request would have been met with strong opposition. Martina's safety was paramount, but T'iang's observations and interactions with the strangers did not raise any cautions. Their intentions seemed sincere. He sensed no animosity or deception from them. In fact, the one thing he did detect was a bond between the couple they themselves were not aware they had. But never one to throw caution to the wind, he instructed his security staff to stay close to his wife and her grandmother in case his instincts failed him.

Upon their arrival in Traveler City, Sylvia met the two strangers and brought them to her grandmother's home. Martina took one look at them and suspected they were special individuals sent by the Goddess for some divine purpose. She warmly welcomed them. After giving the couple a tour of her home and of Traveler City, Martina engaged her visitors in conversation to determine their motives and confirm a gut feeling. She and Sylvia were both empaths so they were sensitive to their guests' feelings.

The couple said they were stranded in the wilderness and needed to find their friends. After careful observation and a few conversations, Martina was convinced their presence was no accident. They talked about being part of a crew of a vehicle from what they called space. The Plains People called it the Great Beyond. The couple said they survived some kind of collision, and crashed on Progensha.

Though most people would have considered their story a wild fantasy, much like Sylvia did, Martina knew otherwise. Based on what they said, and her own experiences and knowledge, Martina determined her guests were not only from the Great Beyond, but also from the future, and unaware they were now living in the past. They had sought help from people they knew from the time they came from not knowing they had been displaced in time. Martina eventually told them they had arrived in Progensha's past. The revelation came as a shock to Lin and Piper.

Once the couple realized they could never return to their time, they slowly accepted their situation and reluctantly assimilated into Progenshan culture, but refused to get involved in the conflict with the Thourons for fear of damaging the timeline and altering the planet's future.

Lin and Piper committed themselves to helping Martina however they could in other ways, which allowed Sylvia to confidently return to the Plains and live with her husband. She was assured her grandmother was in good hands. They proved invaluable when it came to maintaining her archives. Since they were relatively the same age as Sylvia, Martina eventually began referring to them as her grandchildren. And Sylvia was tickled to refer to them as her siblings. In time, Lin and Piper became parents. Lin gave birth to Zuri, and Sylvia became the doting aunt. They were one happy family until Sylvia was mortally wounded at the hands of the Thourons.

With the death of their sister and the loss of their homes in the Grassy Plains, Martina's remaining granddaughters chose to follow their husbands. Being merchants, they decided their best opportunity to continue working at their trades was to live with the Nomads. They did their best to convince their grandmother to come with them, but Martina refused. She insisted on staying put.

Angered by Sylvia's death, Lin and Piper decided they could no longer remain passive observers. They took a more active role in the conflict. As a result, they and Martina, were gravely wounded defending Traveler City against the Thourons. Upon recovery and using their knowledge of the future they helped found and establish the city of Uderra. As a result, countless lives were spared.

When it became evident that Traveler City would fall to the Thourons, Martina insisted on staying in her home. Her decision had angered Lin to the point that she had threatened to bodily remove Martina and drag her kicking and screaming to the relative safety of Uderra until Martina revealed the reason she insisted on staying. After much coaxing, and knowing Lin planned to follow through with her threat to physically remove her from her home, she relented and admitted there was a bomb from the future hidden in a basement bunker in her house. When T'iang suggested taking it with them to Uderra, Martina told them it was impossible to move without guaranteeing it would not be intercepted and captured by the Thourons. As a result, Lin and Piper made the fateful decision to stay and detonate it if they were left with no choice.

Martina wondered if the destruction of the valley was the change to the planet's destiny Lin and Piper feared, but she felt strongly that the same result would have still occurred had she detonated the bomb instead. But at least Lin and Piper would still be alive. Perhaps, their demise is what dooms her world. She decided to do what she could so their sacrifice was not in vain. But her plans would have to wait. Right now she believed she was where she needed to be. With Zuri and T'yree.

Martina's thoughts snapped back to the present when the door to the birthing room opened and a technician stepped out into the hallway. He smiled broadly with a twinkle in his eyes as he looked straight at T'yree and said, "Congratulations. You are the father to a healthy girl."

Martina looked over at T'yree, who looked both proud and terrified.

He gulped, looked up at the man clothed in yellow medical garb and said in a meek voice, "Thank you."

Martina leaned over to peek into the room, softly patted T'yree on his thigh, and said, "A girl? Huh. Somebody really got that wrong. Good luck with that."

Chapter 7

Forty-five sols following the birth of Pyperlyn, and halfway through her maternity leave, Zuri sat in the front room of her home while her daughter slept in a bassinet next to her. She watched a closed circuit videocast of a Uderran High Council meeting on a pad she had on her lap as they discussed and debated what people should do following the destruction of the Grassy Plains.

In the sols leading up to the current convocation, various groups, political and religious leaders campaigned for and sought to motivate their constituents and followers to leave for parts unknown. Many had already left or were in the process of leaving. The meeting was more or less a formality. It was a token gathering of a few council members who still remained. They argued that staying in Uderra was inviting another disaster that could potentially wipe out everyone. All of the wrangling, posturing, and maneuvering resulted in a meeting of the minds and clashing of the strong-willed that culminated in the high council meeting Zuri was watching.

There were heated debates and acerbic rhetoric among the members present in the council chambers. The prevailing sentiment was leaning toward a desire by many to leave Uderra for distant parts of the continent. Far from the destruction zone and as far away from the Thourons as possible. Leading the contingent of those in favor of leaving was a member of the council whose lineage was of Terran, Uderran, and Selemite origin.

Der'von, the third highest ranking member, pressed his point for leaving Uderra to areas he and his cohorts perceived were safer ground.

Known among his people as a savvy negotiator and sagacious leader, Der'von was a gray-skinned man with a muscular build. It was a physique typical of his people and their forebearers. The majority of his ancestors were originally known as Selemites. But two hundred cycles later, they were just another ethnic group among many that made up the citizenry of Uderra.

He had long black hair with a white streak down the center pulled back into a ponytail. Der'von wore a charcoal gray robe with a hood which cradled his hair. As he addressed his colleagues, he gestured with hands that were calloused and scarred, signs of working in the food fields and of his military service to Traveler City and Uderra.

"We must disperse with swiftness to ensure the survival of our people," he said. His voice boomed in the council chamber. "The longer we remain huddled together, the better the chance of our enemy repeating the atrocity against Uderra that was perpetrated in the valley. And I, for one, do not wish to be entrapped when that happens."

Martina, who had sat quietly for most of the proceedings, spoke up and asked, "Don't you mean, if it happens?" She sat across the table facing his empty chair. "And what makes you so certain it was our enemy who ruined the valley?" Martina was by virtue of her family lineage and due to her age, was considered an elder statesman and maintained a permanent seat on the council. She could trace her family tree directly to the original Travelers.

He glared at her first with a look of disbelief that she would ask such questions and then made a derisive noise that sounded more like the snort of a beast of burden from one of the harvest fields. Der'von paused briefly to compose himself before he said, "Oh come now, Lady Martina, who else could it have been? The Thourons are savages who excel at war, division, derision, subterfuge, and destruction. It should be as plain to you as it is to everyone in this room that those warmongers are the cause of the devastation in the valley."

Pyperlyn stirred for a moment drawing her mother's attention as she stretched and yawned then settled back into her blissful sleep. Certain her daughter would not wake up, she turned her attention back to the monitor and studied her great-grandmother intensely.

Martina had a reputation for being obstinate and difficult to coerce. True to her nature, she stood her ground and refused to be intimidated or condescended to.

"What proof do you present as evidence of your claim?" she asked.

Der'von pointed toward the chamber windows and angrily proclaimed with a snarl, "There! Out there is your proof, Lady Martina."

Zuri zoomed in on Martina's face. The woman's expression displayed a sense of calm to those in the room around her, but her great-granddaughter saw a cauldron of anger, disappointment, regret, and something else: defiant determination. The look in her great-grandmother's eyes revealed to no one but Zuri that Martina was planning something.

Der'von returned to his seat and stared at Martina with what looked like contempt in his jet black irises. Martina returned his stare until he looked away. Zuri was not certain, but she thought she saw consternation in his eyes. She was impressed. Her great-grandmother had managed to unnerve Der'von.

Other members of the council spoke when called upon, and all were in agreement with Der'von. Each said they were considering leaving Uderra for parts unknown. And Martina argued with each one to convince them to stay. No one was willing to. It appeared that her great-grandmother was pushing a boulder uphill.

Another council member, Lolaan, whose ethnic mix included dominant traits of Felid ancestry, had silky red body hair, long whiskers, and slender paws and tail, echoed Der'von's position, but with much less abrasiveness. She took a more diplomatic approach.

"Lady Martina," she began. She nearly purred it. "No one here is one hundred percent certain who is directly responsible for what happened. But the prevailing sentiment is if it were not for the Thourons waging war upon us, this horrific tragedy may never have happened. You cannot fault us for at least thinking it."

"Yes, yes." Another council member said.

The comment was followed by a few murmurs of support by others before Lolaan said, "I recommend we put it to a vote. Those who vote to leave, shall be permitted to do so. And those who vote to stay, shall be free to stay."

She puffed her cheeks and twitched her tail as more murmurs floated around the chamber. Lolaan let the delegates discuss and debate before she spoke again.

"And I propose to allow the populace to have a voice in this debate, as it is their lives and livelihoods that will be most affected by whatever we decide."

"And our constituents will be free to follow whoever they wish," Der'von added.

Martina backed her wheelchair away from the table and proceeded to roll around the room. She deliberately faced each council member silently challenging them before she spoke her mind. A cold, icy tone dripped from her words.

"Esteemed colleagues, it is obvious you all have made up your minds to abandon all that you hold sacred. All that you love. All that you swore to uphold and protect. All that you worked so hard to build these last twenty cycles. That is abundantly clear to me and everyone in attendance." She paused before continuing. "I get it. I really do. And I get that you feel we are vulnerable if we stay together, but I ask you, how much more vulnerable will you be once you have removed yourselves from the safety of Uderra?"

"Less vulnerable than we are now," replied one.

"But there is safety in our collective numbers rather than apart," Martina shot back.

"It is also safer not to contain all our unhatched in one clutch," said another.

Martina was normally unflappable, but frustration manifested itself on her face as she pursed her lips and raised her eyes toward the chamber ceiling before she exhaled a deep and audible sigh.

Martina sensed there was nothing she could do or say that would sway the others from going ahead with their plans. She was frustrated beyond frustration, but she accepted defeat and said in an even tone, "So be it." She wheeled herself back to her station at the table.

Feeling resolute in their apparent victory, those who were determined to leave began to discuss exit strategies when they were interrupted by Martina as she theatrically cleared her throat.

"Since it is obvious that I cannot persuade you to reconsider, would you all be inclined to allow me to assist you with your exodus? I have," she purposely hesitated before she finished saying, "resources you may find useful. I respectfully offer my services."

Shocked at her request and offer, the chamber reverberated with suspiciously hushed murmurs as the other members discussed Martina's request. When the murmuring quieted down, Der'von stood and said, "The majority consensus in this chamber is to leave Uderra with great haste, as many already have. However, I am willing to consider your request if what you offer will be of significant benefit to those participating in the *exodus*." He spoke the last word of the sentence with great emphasis.

She said, "Wise of you to accept. You have no idea how significant I can be. The success of your endeavors will be contingent upon what I can offer you."

Der'von snorted and said, "With all due respect, Lady Martina, I seriously doubt that."

Martina sniffed and with a derisive lilt in her voice said, "We shall see."

There was not much that unnerved Der'von, but Zuri could see Martina's tone pierced the man's defenses.

You're planning something, gran. What do you have in your bag of tricks? Zuri wondered.

Chapter 8

Following the council meeting, Martina and T'yree returned home. Zuri, having watched the proceedings, knew her great-grandmother was highly agitated. She pretended not to know what transpired.

"How'd it go, Gran?"

"How'd it go? How'd it go?"

Martina huffed before she answered the question. "Not as well as I had hoped. They're afraid—and rightfully so. They believe that what happened in the valley could happen here in Uderra."

"Understandable."

"Understandable? Yes. Warranted? No."

"What makes you so certain?"

Before Martina answered the question she huffed again then waved off T'yree who was still holding her wheelchair. He backed off, looked at the two women and decided it would be wiser to be somewhere else. He left the house as quickly as he could.

They both watched him as he slipped out the front door and gingerly closed it as if pulling harder on it would cause the house to crumble.

Zuri repeated her question. "So what makes you so certain their fear is unwarranted?"

"Because I know things they don't."

"What things?"

"Things."

Martina was unwilling to answer the question so Zuri switched tactics. "Don't tell me you told them you had a vision from the Goddess."

There was an almost imperceptible hesitation in Martina's voice before she said, "No."

"Are you being honest with me, Gran?"

Martina hesitated again before she said, "Yes."

It was apparent her great-grandmother was hiding something.

"Then what is the issue that is bothering you? If they wish to leave, they should be able to do so freely. They're afraid for themselves and for their people."

"I understand that. What they don't understand is their fears are unfounded. But they are unwilling to listen to the voice of reason."

"Yours?"

"Yes, mine."

Martina snapped her reply with a vehement forcefulness Zuri had never heard.

Zuri waited a beat before she continued questioning her great-grandmother.

"So why would you think that any of them would listen to anything you had to say if what you have to say is counter to what they want to do?"

"Because I know more than they do about what happened and why."

"And just how is it that you know more than they do?"

Martina knew that she had said much more than she should have to Zuri so she tried to deflect the young woman's curious questions and accusatory stare and fell back on the one thing she believed Zuri would not question. Her religious convictions.

"Because I had an epiphany from the Goddess Herself."

Zuri's response dripped with sarcasm and suspicion.

"Really?"

Martina's response reflected what sounded like hurt feelings and an irritated disbelief that her great-granddaughter would question her integrity.

"Now you doubt me?"

Despite being an empath, it was sometimes difficult to read Zuri's feelings. Her great-granddaughter had learned to control and block her emotions from being detected. Martina counted on Zuri believing her because she was aware her great-granddaughter perceived her to be a deeply religious person. It worked. Sort of.

Zuri changed her tone to something that sounded more empathetic, but was underscored by a bit of barely detectable sarcasm.

"No, I don't doubt you. I believe you saw what you felt you saw."

"Now you mock me?"

Martina was trying to throw Zuri off balance and believed it worked when she detected the confusion and shame Zuri felt before her great-granddaughter regained control and repaired the cracks in the wall she constructed to block her emotions from being probed.

In a more contrite tone Zuri sighed and said, "No, Gran. I would never do that. I respect and understand the deep bond you have with the Goddess."

This time Zuri's response was sincere. She made an earnest attempt to defuse an emotional powder keg that threatened to explode resulting in the uninviting atmosphere T'yree wisely chose to escape from.

"Good. Never forget that. Swear to it."

Zuri looked Martina squarely in her eyes and said, "I swear I will never forget the deep relationship you have with the Goddess."

They held each other's gaze before Zuri looked away. She unintentionally let slip another feeling of emotional weakness. She was genuinely embarrassed that she dropped her guard, giving Martina the opportunity to peek into her feelings. If there was one lesson she learned from her mother, it was to resist any attempts by your opponent to force you into a situation where you reveal your vulnerabilities. In this instance, she failed.

Martina sensed the confusion in the young woman's feelings and was satisfied she had successfully discombobulated her great-granddaughter.

“Good. Now let me tell you why I believe I’m right.”

Martina planned to appeal to Zuri’s sense of logic rather than to her emotions. At least, she thought, it would reduce the volatility currently putting them at odds with each other. If her plan was going to work, she would need her great-granddaughter on her side.

Chapter 9

"So you're saying the solution to their concerns lies within the archives you've amassed?"

"Yes."

"But that's just a dusty old collection of useless archaic junk that serves no purpose but to entertain nostalgists."

"Dusty, archaic junk you said you were interested in looking at."

"Because mother and father said it made for interesting reading, and because they told me they added to it and I might find it enlightening."

"Did they give you any details?"

"No," Zuri lied. "They just said it contained information about where they came from before they arrived in Traveler City, and some personal insight about the war."

Pyperlyn stirred in her bassinet. Zuri rocked it until her daughter settled back into a restful sleep. She gazed at her daughter for a moment and wondered what kind of life a half-Terran, half-Progenshan child would have living in a world torn apart quite literally by war and hate.

"Well," Martina began, "You may be surprised at what you will find. Your parents made me swear to never divulge the information to you. They wanted to tell you themselves when they thought you would be old enough to understand." Martina exhaled a remorseful sigh. "Unfortunately, they never got the chance."

"They never got the chance to tell me in person, but they will posthumously in the archives in their own words." A small glimmer of hope slipped through Zuri's carefully crafted facade. Knowing she would read her parents' thoughts or hear their words caused her to lower her guard.

Martina sensed her great-granddaughter's excitement and felt a pang of remorse and guilt. Remorse for the loss of Lin and Piper. Guilt for letting them talk her out of doing what they ultimately did.

Following a brief pause in their conversation, Martina said, “Give me a micton. I’ll be right back.” Then she rolled her wheelchair to her room.

Zuri could hear noises that sounded like Martina was rummaging through her things looking for something. She had never been in her great-grandmother’s room because she kept it locked, so she could only imagine what it looked like. After what was several mictons later, Martina emerged with a small data pad in her hand.

“Here.” She held the pad out to Zuri. “Take this. It’s from your parents. They gave it to me when I evacuated Traveler City. They said if anything happened to them, I was to give it to you when the time was right.”

Martina’s hand trembled slightly as Zuri reached for the pad and took it from her great-grandmother.

“I believe this time is as good as any,” Martina said.

Zuri held the device reverently in her hands, clutched it against her chest and, with tears in her eyes, whispered, “Thank you.”

Then she just froze. She held the tablet as still as a statue.

“Well, are you going to turn it on or cry all over it?”

After a moment’s hesitation, Zuri turned it on and saw and heard her parents. They had solemn expressions on their faces and their voices sounded weary.

Hi, Munchkin, her mother said, *if you’re seeing this that means we’re with the Goddess now. We asked Martina to give this to you when we were gone. We both love you very much. And we’re sorry we won’t be there when your child is born. But don’t worry. You’ll be a terrific mother.*

Lin’s voice faltered so Piper put an arm around his wife to console her before he spoke up.

We know you’ll have a bunch of questions so we recorded a sort of a journal for you. Since the sol you were born, we’ve been recording things about us and about things we think you should know. Listen to Martina. She will be able to help. Okay, Munchkin, we gotta go. We love you.

They blew kisses at the screen before it went dark. That was a gut-wrenching tease. Zuri just sat motionless looking at the dark screen. Not moving. Not speaking. Not even crying. She did not know quite how to feel. There was something about the video that bothered her. It was as if a sixth sense kicked in. Something triggered a subconscious alert, but she could not pin down why. Her mother always told her to listen to her gut feelings, and right now they were screaming at her.

Martina sensed her great-granddaughter's confusion, and after an excruciating moment of silence, said, "Call your husband and tell him to get back here to watch his daughter. I need you to go with me to the vault. I will show you where your parents' records are stored, and I will reveal to you my plan for the future of the planet."

Future of the planet?

That was the furthest thing from Zuri's mind.

The timing could not have been more ideal since she was midway through her leave. Now that Martina decided to grant her access to the vault, she would have more time to discover what was contained in it.

While Zuri and Martina talked and made plans, T'yree spent his time driving around Uderra in the family chariot. He was not taking in the sites, but was visiting the various sectors observing and taking note of what was being done in preparation for what was now referred to on the news feeds officially as the Exodus. Almost as soon as the council meeting ended, the packing began in earnest.

People were loading up chariots, trucks, and anything with wheels with their possessions. They were preparing to head out to places unknown. He was driving through the Selemite sector when his in-dash communicator beeped. He gave it a quick glance and saw that his wife was calling. He answered.

"Yes, my sweet, is it safe for me to return home?"

"Very funny. Of course it is safe for you to come home. I wouldn't be calling otherwise." She paused. "I need you to do something for me."

Of course there was a catch. Where his wife was concerned, there always was a catch. She was a lot like her great-grandmother.

“What do you wish for me to do so that the list of things you owe me will continue to get longer?”

Zuri replied with a term her mother sometimes used when her parents would bicker, “Bite me.” Then she asked him if he would watch Pyperlyn while she and Martina visited the vault. He said he would as he wove through traffic on his way home.

Chapter 10

Nadir, Andorra, and Naron all sat in a cramped debriefing room along with their unit as its commanders digested the reports the three of them gave.

"It appears our enemy was a lot more cunning and savage than we thought. We must strike back with superior efficiency," said the senior officer who was in charge of overseeing the briefing. He was a lanky man with bony fingers, considerably older than nearly everyone in the room, and set in his ways. His expression reflected annoyance when he was interrupted by Nadir.

"We do not know for certain that it was our enemy that caused the destruction," Nadir said. "It could have been from someone else who is attempting to manipulate us into a trap."

Nadir did not believe for one micton the Plains People, the Travelers, or the Uderrans were capable of doing what was done. He also thought that whatever happened, there was too much at stake for them to just blow it all up. There had to be a rational explanation. One that was not readily apparent.

The officer sneered derisively at Nadir. "Surely you would not have us believe it was someone else," he said. "There is no one else. Those savages maliciously massacred Thouron soldiers to deprive us of our divine right to rule this world."

Nadir made another attempt to mitigate the crescendo of hatred building up in the room.

"All I am saying is the intelligence I have been able to gather thus far is not definitive. None of them point toward our adversaries. The weapon that was used is beyond anything they are capable of."

The senior officer directed all of his attention and venom toward Nadir.

"Did it ever occur to you that your information may have been flawed? And since when have you been so concerned with the accuracy of your reports? You report, we decide. To otherwise question those reports or what we decide to do with them could indicate you're turning soft. Are you turning soft?"

The attention of every soldier in the room was focused on Nadir. He swallowed hard at the insinuation. The question was more of an accusation of something else, but before he said something that would alter everyone's perspective of him, Andorra, who was sitting next to him, dug a very sharp fingernail into his thigh. No one but he knew what she had done. It took a great deal of concentration and effort not to wince. She had jabbed him rather hard.

“No, Commandant, I was simply trying to be thorough in light of this unprecedented calamity. There has been nothing like it in the history of our world.”

The senior officer, after a slight hesitation, seemed to consider the statement. When he appeared to be satisfied with Nadir’s response, he continued to berate their foes and repeat practiced and ingrained clichés deriding their enemies and promoting the Thouron doctrine of natural superiority and manifest destiny. The tension in the room eased, replaced with one of enthusiastic repugnance for non-Thourons.

When the briefing was over and everyone was dismissed, Nadir left without waiting for his friends. When they caught up with him, Naron grabbed Nadir’s shoulder and demanded to know, “What was that drat back there?”

Nadir shook off Naron’s hand and asked, “What was what?” as he continued to walk.

“What do you mean, ‘What was what?’ What was that near insubordination drat? You came real close to sounding unpatriotic.”

Nadir stopped midstride, whirled toward Naron and said, “How dare you question my patriotism.”

It was not phrased as a question. Nadir closed the space between them and got close to his friend’s face then asked a question that was more of a demand.

“After everything I have done for our people, and you stand there and question my loyalty?”

Surprised by the ferociousness of Nadir’s indignant challenge, Naron stepped back, swallowed, and said with less bravado, “It sounded like it.” He eyed his friend with cautious curiosity.

“What things sound like and what they appear to be are not always what they actually are. That is why I am in intelligence and you are not.” The insult was clear.

Naron glared at Nadir then said, "I thought I knew you. But maybe I don't know you as well as I thought." He made a crisp about-face and walked away without saying another word.

Nadir turned his attention to Andorra. "Do you question my loyalty as well?"

She looked at him with eyes that matched the hue of Progensha's peach sky but revealed nothing about the thoughts behind them.

"What I question," she said in an even tone of voice, "is your judgement and your sanity. You have not been yourself since the cataclysm. I pray that you find your center and your path before you are completely lost. I suspect you have reached a crossroads in your life and are questioning your very purpose. And perhaps the Goddess Herself. A few now are. Do not lose sight of who you were, who you are, and who you want to become."

"What do you mean?"

He searched her stoic features for some sign of an emotional cue. He saw none.

"I mean that all of us have been changed in some way by what happened. Some more profoundly than others."

She stepped closer and leaned into his personal space until their faces nearly touched. Then she lowered her voice to a near whisper. To Nadir, it sounded like an angry whisper. Anyone looking at them would have guessed she was giving him an unsolicited and unwanted piece of her mind. His body language would have reinforced that assumption.

"As someone who deals with information that is fleeting and can be easily manipulated and misrepresented, one could surmise you have reached a threshold in your life where you have begun to question the motives of those who take those facts and mold them into things that are dangerously deceptive and indistinguishable from the truth. The consequences of such insidious manipulations have lasting consequences."

Even though it looked like she could not get closer, she did and lowered the tone of her voice to that of a half whisper while continuing to hold his gaze.

"I believe you no longer feel like an indispensable asset but more like an expendable tool in an endless war that has seen many innocents die as a result of the information you supplied. A cog in a perpetually spinning wheel. I know the destruction of the vale has affected you deeply. I could tell from your behavior on the overlook."

"Am I that transparent?"

Andorra took a step back, but did not change the tone or inflection of her voice.

"To me, yes. But you forget, we are in the same profession. Trained to see things as they really are, not as someone else wants them to be seen. If you are not careful, others not so … insightful or forgiving will see your misgivings as signs of weakness and use them to your disadvantage. You risk *disappearing* as so many others have."

He eyed her suspiciously before he asked, "Are you my enemy now?"

She did not answer.

Uncertain of her motives, he asked, "Why did you jab me with your finger?"

All she said was, "You seek enlightenment and redemption from the Goddess. You will not find it where you think. Be mindful of both your words and your actions. Tread lightly."

Andorra studied him for a moment before she said, "We are more of a kindred spirit than you realize."

Her face remained impassive, but Nadir saw the hint of something in her eyes before she stepped back, turned, and walked away. What that something was inexplicably filled him with questions and feelings of dread.

He watched as she turned a corner and disappeared from view. In just a few brief mictons he sensed their relationship had changed.

Chapter 11

On T'yree's return trip home, he had the time to ponder his wife's request that he watch Pyperlyn while she went with Lady Martina to the vault. He was slightly miffed. Why should he be saddled with watching their daughter while Zuri and her great-grandmother went to the vault? It was not because he thought watching their daughter was a chore or punishment. He relished any time he could spend with her, but he had asked to also be permitted access to the vault. And there was no way they were going to leave him alone to care for Pyperlyn while they went down to the bowels of the complex. They would all go and share responsibility for watching their daughter. This, after all, was going to be their maiden adventure, and by the Goddess he was not going to miss it.

He opened the front door to their home prepared to argue his case and was surprised to see his daughter sleeping peacefully in her bassinet, but there was no sign of Zuri or Lady Martina. A light heat flushed his cheeks until he heard voices coming from Martina's room. A moment later, his wife emerged from the room. She stopped short upon seeing him and said, "Took you long enough."

Martina followed behind Zuri, looked him up and down before she asked, "Are you ready?"

All he did was gawk at them before he said, "I thought you intended to leave me with our daughter when you knew I wanted to be included."

Martina scoffed at him. "If you know anything about me it should be that I am a woman of my word."

"Yeah," Zuri agreed. "Now hurry up and get our daughter so we can get this field trip started." She slung a bag over her shoulders filled with baby supplies then grabbed Martina's wheelchair and started for the door. She looked over her shoulder and asked, "Are you coming or not?"

He gently lifted Pyperlyn from her bassinet so as to not wake her, secured her in a stroller kept by the front door, and followed his wife and Martina out for the short walk to the vault.

They passed construction crews and soldiers along the way. The expansion of the city's fortifications had taken on a sense of urgency following the cataclysm. A myriad of construction projects were in various stages of completion. One of those many projects was a massive effort to enlarge and expand the footprint of the royal palace above and below ground. The goal was to connect it to the excavation work being done to the underground facility already under construction.

Ten mictons later, they approached a remote area away from the organized chaos. In one corner of a plot of empty land stood what looked like a rapidly assembled guard shack.

As the little group approached the guard house, one of the two guards saw them coming and whacked her sleeping companion awake. Annoyed that she had disrupted his slumber, he snorted with a snide tone of dissatisfaction before he started to protest, “What in the Goddess …?” His complaint trailed off when he saw who approached. Fully awake and alert, both guards snapped to attention and greeted their visitors with the Uderran salute of respect with both arms crossed in front of their chests.

Zuri wheeled Martina up to the gate and said, “At ease, troopers. There is no need to strain a muscle on our account.” She could tell these two were fresh out of the academy. This posting was probably their first assignment. And they looked fearful that she would report them because they were sleeping on the job—sort of. “Get used to seeing us,” Zuri told them. She delighted in their confused expressions.

“Yes, ma’am,” they said in unison.

Zuri handed over their IDs. The young female verified their credentials then nodded to her companion to let them through. He raised the makeshift gate by hand to let their visitors through so they could get to an elevator that would take them down to the vault.

Martina placed her thumb on a pad by the elevator doors to gain access. When the vault was constructed, Martina had insisted on the highest level of security. She wanted retinal and DNA confirmation. To her chagrin, what she got was a minimum level. The designers were going to automate the process because she, Lin, and Piper were the only ones who used it. But Martina put up such a fuss, that the High Council caved and stationed guards. What annoyed Martina was the guards they assigned were the lowest rank palace guards. Needless to say, being relegated to the area farthest away from everything was not their favorite duty assignment.

They rode the elevator to the lowest level and stepped out into what looked like a heavily fortified bunker surrounded by walls of dirt.

Martina muttered to herself, “They could have at least reinforced the walls so they don’t collapse around the vault.”

“Well,” Zuri began, “if something happens and the walls do collapse, at least no one will be able to get to the vault because no one will know it’s even here.”

Martina snorted with disgust in her voice. “I have a plan in case that ever happens.”

“I’m sure you do, Gran.”

“You bet I do.”

“Ladies, shall we stay on task?” T’yree asked. He attempted to distract the two women from meandering into a snipe session.

“You are quite right,” Martina said. “We must stay on task.” She wheeled herself over to two large steel doors that looked ominous in the dim lighting that illuminated the area surrounding the vault. Martina punched in a code on a keypad adjacent to the right door then waited as a thunk then a click was heard behind both doors before they slid into the walls like pocket doors. “Shall we?” she asked.

Chapter 12

Despite the dismal atmosphere surrounding the vault, the inside was the exact opposite. Everything was arranged in neat orderly rows of shelves, cabinets, clearly labeled boxes, and comfortable computer workstations. Even the air was comfortably cool.

Zuri let out a low whistle, which signaled she was amazed.

T'yree pushed Pyperlyn's stroller over to a long metal table the color of metal gray and simply said, "Impressive."

"The Uderran Corps of Engineers did the digging out down here, your parents organized everything," Martina said. "If it wasn't for them, this place would've looked like my house did."

"Cluttered," Zuri said.

"Lived in," Martina retorted. "And I seem to recall a certain little girl who loved to hide amongst the so-called clutter."

A flash memory of playing hiding games with her parents popped into Zuri's mind. She smiled at the pleasant memory. Then, just to be contrary, replied, "Whatever." She winked at her great-grandmother to signal the playfulness of their banter. T'yree watched in amused silence.

Before the construction of the vault, Martina stored everything in her home. Lin, Piper, and T'iang helped with moving her archives to the vault before the destruction of Traveler City and the valley.

"I never saw any of the schematics or plans for this place," Zuri mused.

"Because only I, T'iang, and your parents worked on and designed this repository. I made them swear an oath they never tell anyone about it—including you. The UCE team was a special classified unit. They were under orders to keep this secret. A few select members of the royal family know this place exists. And that's how it's going to stay. Do I make myself clear?"

Martina plastered a stern look on her face with the implied threat that if others outside of those already in the know found out, their access to the vault would be revoked, and its existence denied.

Zuri spoke for both of them when she said, “Yes, Gran, we heard you loud and clear.”

She could sense they were sincere in their affirmations. T’yree’s feelings were freely accessible and Zuri did not appear to have any emotional blocks engaged. “Good. Now let’s get you two set up.”

Martina pointed toward a nearby multi-user workstation and motioned for them to sit down. Zuri sat on one side of the workstation while T’yree sat on the opposite side. They placed the stroller between them at the end of the table. Zuri continued to take in her surroundings.

The vault was completely self contained. It drew its power from nearby geothermal vents. No power from the surface was required. It was climate controlled and hermetically sealed to help reduce degradation of the data stored within. Zuri surmised as long as there was no breach, the information stored there could last indefinitely.

Martina watched Zuri give the place a critical examination from the perspective of an engineer.

“Despite what you see up top, or on the other side of the main doors, everything here is precisely controlled,” Martina said. “This entire vault is self-contained. It has its own power generator below us. Powered by thermal vents deeper underground.”

The aisles were wide enough for Martina to zip around in her wheelchair. The shelves were designed to raise and lower with the push of a button or pull of a lever. The illumination was more than adequate to allow someone to do research on hard copy material without damaging the integrity of the archival pieces with harsh lights.

Once her guests were settled, Martina whipped her chair around a corner then returned a little while later with a couple of boxes of data discs on her lap. She gestured for Zuri to take one and T’yree to take the other.

“Here. These should be enough to get you started. When you’re done, file them back in their proper locations. Got that?”

“Yes, Gran.”

“Yes, Lady Martina.”

"And how many times do I have to tell you? Stop calling me Lady Martina." She glared at T'yree.

"Yes, my Lady." He smirked at her. His training would not permit him to address her as anything else. So whenever she insisted he not use her title, he simply shortened it. She huffed before rolling back into the rows of shelves. She was on a private mission.

True to her word, Martina had brought out data discs for Zuri that her parents had recorded for her, and she brought discs for T'yree that covered the early sols when his people first encountered the Travelers.

Eager to get started, Zuri rolled up her sleeves, inserted a wireless earpiece for private listening, grabbed a disc labeled Disc One, and inserted it into the workstation. Her husband did the same with his box, and they began their respective journeys through time.

Chapter 13

The first thing Zuri saw appear on the screen was a video image of her parents smiling and waving at the camera. They appeared to be looking at and speaking directly to her as if they were still all together. And they were unbelievably young looking. She immediately got a chill and teared up.

Hi, Munchkin, her mother began. *Hope everything is going well for you. Your father and I decided to make some recordings to tell you a little something about ourselves. Hopefully, when you're old enough, these vids will make sense.*

Maybe after you see these vids, you'll understand why we told you not to tell anyone that we're not from Progensha, and why we also said to keep that our little secret. Gran and uncle T are the only other people who know, but we don't want them to know you know. Hopefully, you'll understand when you're older.

Lin paused for a secton and looked at Piper before continuing. Her voice cracked as she tried to stifle a sniffle.

The main reason we decided to record these vids was to explain things to you in case we're not around anymore. Because of the war, we're never sure if we will have a chance to tell you the full story in person when you get old enough. So if you're seeing this without us, we're most likely not around anymore. That's why we made these recordings. We have a lot to tell you. Hopefully, when we're finished, you'll know us better—and maybe yourself too.

Zuri felt another chill and a pang of loss. She paused the playback until she regained her composure. Her attention was momentarily diverted by a foul stench in the air. Pyperlyn needed a diaper change. Zuri stole a surreptitious side-eye toward T'yree. He was doing his best pretending not to look at his wife or smell the air, but he failed miserably. He could never have a career as a spy. And as for diaper changing, they were going to have a little talk. She was not going to be the only one to change their daughter's soiled undies. She did not say a word, made it obvious by huffing, sighing, and growling, that she was not pleased with diaper duty.

Once she finished changing Pyperlyn, and made a theatrical display of slam dunking the diaper into the disposal pail, she handed their daughter to him so he could feed her.

Zuri resumed video playback. She saw her mother turn to her father and ask, *So where should we begin?*

Let's start with our childhoods and go from there, Piper said. *I'll go first.*

Okay with me.

Piper talked about being born on a planet called Terra Prime and that he was fortunate enough to grow up in a wealthy family. He quickly glossed over his childhood. He said it was boring. He went to elite schools, had hoity-toity friends, and overbearing parents. His siblings were all interested in climbing the social ladder, and did not care who they stepped on to get to the top. He, on the other hand, wanted to make a difference in people's lives.

Because there was a galactic war raging, he saw joining the military as his way of making that difference. So he enlisted in the military and trained in medicine at the academy. His family tried to dissuade him from pursuing his endeavor. It wasn't noble enough, they said. They felt military service was for the lower class. It was beneath him. He told them he believed it was his calling. They threatened to cut off his inheritance if he insisted on following the path he chose. He insisted. As a result, he was cut off from the family. Disowned. He pretty much told them what they could do with themselves and continued serving.

I felt I had to stay true to my heart, Piper said.

He summarized his life in the academy then jokingly talked about how he met her mother purely by accident. He, a few classmates, and their instructors were on a mission to deliver much needed supplies to a few frontier colony worlds when their relief ship was attacked. They crashed on a remote planet and did their best to survive until help arrived. Unfortunately, much of the animal life was predatory and devastated their party. Out of a group of forty survivors, ten remained after being stranded for eight months. Piper said it was dumb luck they were even found.

A space battle took place above the planet and two pilots crashed near his encampment. The pilots had been exposed to poisonous snake blood and were dying. He and a few of his classmates found the pilots and saved them with an antidote they synthesized. They were all found and eventually rescued when a search party, sent to look for the pilots, discovered everybody.

The officer in charge of the rescue party was your mother, he said. *Well, she wasn't your mother then because we had just met, but you know what I mean. We sorta connected afterwards and the rest, as they say, is history.*

Lin whacked him on his shoulder and said, *It didn't happen quite like that.* She appeared to think about it before she said, *Well, it kinda did happen like that.* She turned back toward the camera and picked up where Piper left off.

Anyway, he and the other cadets got a clean bill of health from the medics and promotions from the ship's captain. Then we sorta started hanging around each other, and the rest is history.

Lin prattled on about shipboard duties and responsibilities before she started telling Zuri about her early life living on a planet called Ventura IV.

There isn't much to tell, she began. Lin paused as she thought about what she was going to say, then continued on. *I had what you could say was an average life. My father died when I was very young. I have vague memories of him.*

Lin proceeded to talk about growing up on Ventura IV with her best friend and how they were going to Ventura University together until her colony world was attacked and she became a casualty of war. She lost her mother and her best friend and the only family she had left. After she recovered from her injuries, she joined the military and became a security officer.

Zuri was fascinated with the stories, but was also feeling fatigued. She could barely keep her eyes open. T'yree had already surrendered to sleep. They would continue tomorrow and the sols after. It was not surprising that Martina had fallen asleep before T'yree did considering the sol she had.

Zuri stopped the playback and woke her husband and great-grandmother. They gathered their archival material, gathered their daughter, and made their way home.

Chapter 14

The next sol, Zuri awoke to the smell of breakfast wafting into the bedroom. With eyes still closed, she reached behind her to feel for T'yree and got the confirmation she expected. He had awakened before her and had started cooking breakfast. Despite having royal chefs available to fix their meals, he insisted on doing all the cooking. Which was fine by her because she hated cooking. She did not care who did the cooking as long as it was not her. Through squinted eyes, she reached toward the bassinet next to her to check on Pyperlyn and saw she was not in it.

Good, she thought, *at least he took it upon himself to take more responsibility for our daughter without being told.*

Zuri slid out of bed and headed straight for the bathroom. Once refreshed, she was ready to begin the sol. She scanned her military wardrobe and chose something not too stringent, but subtle enough to remind the young soldiers guarding the vault she was not just a casual user. She did not want to intimidate them, but to remind them they were there for a very serious reason. Zuri settled on a one-piece jumpsuit with just the right shade of dirt brown. It was comfortable and reflected her position in the military and royal hierarchy. Once dressed, she headed to the front room where T'yree was feeding himself and Pyperlyn.

"Nice of you to finally join us," he said.

"You can't rush greatness," she said.

"You flatter yourself too much."

"You don't flatter me enough," she teased.

Before sitting down to eat, Zuri kissed her husband lightly on the lips and her daughter on her forehead. She grabbed a fork and jabbed at her food then shoveled it into her mouth. She stopped chewing, savored the taste then patted the table with her hand a few times. "Blessed be the Goddess. You've outdone yourself–or I'm really hungry." She took a few more bites then said, with an obvious grin on her face, "I think I'm really hungry."

"Mud boar droppings," he said. "You know you like it. I'm the best cook in all of Uderra."

Her grin transformed into a full smile. "Yes," she said reluctantly. "You quite possibly are the best in all of the land."

They traded playful jabs at each other while they ate, then Zuri held their daughter for a while. She marvelled at how small she was, and wondered if she would experience the growth spurt Uderran children went through. After ten cycles, Uderran children were fully grown adults. Physically, mentally, and emotionally. Unlike T'yree, Zuri was a full Terran and therefore grew up according to Terran standards. She was at least ten cycles older than her husband, although they were relatively the same age by Uderran standards. Time would tell when it came to Pyperlyn.

T'yree cleared their dishes and put them into the washer prompting Zuri to ask about Martina.

"Lady Martina got an early start on the sol. She fixed herself a bit to eat then requested a military escort to the vault. She left a message saying something about finishing what she started."

"Finishing what she started," Zuri repeated. "I wonder what she meant by that."

"With that woman? Only the Goddess knows."

"And maybe even the Goddess Herself doesn't know."

T'yree chuckled. "You may be right."

Together, they put away all evidence of their morning refreshment, and after a brief lecture from Zuri, when the pungent aroma of the morning meal made it clear the nourishment had made its way through Pyperlyn, T'yree changed her diaper.

Dressed, groomed, and nutritionally satisfied, they prepared to head to the vault. After T'yree packed them lunch, and Zuri bundled Pyperlyn into her stroller, they left their compound and took the short walk to the archives. The construction work was going on further from their living quarters. City planners were busy hollowing out the underground preparing to build an elaborate complex that would house healing and military facilities.

When they approached the two guards assigned to vault duty, both soldiers were alert and prepared to receive them as they each stood at attention.

"Greetings, Lady Lin-Piper and Lord T'yree," the male half of the duo said. There was a detectable nervous twinge in his voice. "Please present your credentials for verification."

Zuri and T'yree handed over their IDs and waited for the guard to scan them. His hands trembled as he accepted their IDs and attempted to insert them into the data verifier. He dropped both cards then scrambled to scoop them up from off the ground. He blew off the dirt then wiped their cards on his uniform to clean up any dust residue before making a second attempt to verify their credentials.

Zuri felt sorry for the struggling guard and made the effort to sooth his frayed nerves when she said, "We don't bite, trooper." She detected a slight relaxation in his movements. He was able to complete the verification, handed them back their IDs and wished them a good sol.

The female guard unlocked the gate and raised it so they could pass through. She never said a word and barely made eye contact. For one brief moment she looked directly at Zuri with nervous eyes, and relaxed slightly when she saw her flash an almost imperceptible smile. The young soldier returned the gesture with a traditional Uderran salute.

Martina had them both cleared to use the elevator. So Zuri summoned it. When it arrived, Zuri and T'yree stepped on with their daughter and disappeared behind the closed doors to the guards' relief.

Looking straight ahead at the doors as the elevator descended, T'yree said, "You looked like you took great pleasure in the guards' discomfort."

Without turning her head, Zuri cocked an eye in his direction and said, "No. Not really. I remember when I was like them. A bundle of nerves trying to impress my superior officers without coming across looking like an academy cadet. Afraid I was going to get a foot up my ass for doing something wrong."

"So you weren't getting any pleasure from seeing them sweat?"

"Well, maybe a little."

"Now that's the Zuri I know."

"Bite me."

The low hum of the elevator stopped as it reached the vault. The doors slid open, and the family stepped out into the cavernous space that was the archives. Pyperlyn had fallen asleep on the trip over and remained that way when they approached the workstation. The sounds of Martina rifling through whatever she was doing came from the deeper recesses of the chamber. No doubt implementing part of her secret plan, Zuri thought.

Chapter 15

Zuri sat at her side of the workstation and resumed watching the video from the sol before.

Lin recounted her time in the military, her promotions, and the names of people she heard her parents mention as a child growing up. There were two electronic entities called Cora and Sojourner. Then there were Markka, Sparks, Raqmar, Vee, and David Leahcim, the brother of her best friend. In an obvious display of teasing Piper, Lin leaned in close to the screen, covered the side of her mouth with one hand, and whispered how she once had a youthful romantic interest in her friend's brother. Zuri heard her father's voice from offscreen say, *I can still hear you, you know.* Lin sat back and in her normal tone said, *Of course all of that was before I met your father. The one true love of my life.*

Then she saw her father slide into view and plant a passionate kiss squarely on her mother's lips. Zuri could see Lin's hand wave across the screen reaching for something before it suddenly went blank.

Zuri blinked a few times and wondered what went wrong before it dawned on her what happened. She smiled and cringed. There were many times after she reached the age of majority her parents would ask, 'How do you think you got here?' Her thoughts drifted to the intimate moments she and T'yree shared before Pyperlyn was born and all of the times since. She smiled again, but this time it was with the understanding of a wife and lover. A moment later, the playback started up again.

Her parents both reappeared looking a bit disheveled and much more relaxed.

Sorry about that, Munchkin, something came up that we had to, uh, take care of. Now where were we? Oh yeah. I remember now.

Lin and Piper took turns describing how a motley group of people became a tightly knit group of close friends who eventually became a family. It was that familial relationship that kept them going after they were stranded on Progensha. It was their determination to survive and a brush with death following an attack by a dart lizard that strengthened the bond between them.

Just as her parents began to talk about what transpired, Martina appeared with a couple of large metal security crates filled with archival material on a dolly tied to the back of her chair. She towed them into the viewing room.

T'yree immediately sprang up to help her.

"What have we here?" Zuri asked.

"Some things those headstrong twits will need on their *exodus* from Uderra." She made quotation marks with her fingers to emphasize the word.

"Like what?"

"Survival know-how and whatnot."

"Care to elaborate?"

"No."

"Alrighty then. I guess we're done here."

"For now."

T'yree watched, head swiveling from one woman to the other as if watching a sporting event.

"T'yree?"

"Yes, Lady Martina."

She bristled at being addressed as Lady. "Please put this dolly by the elevator for me. Then call and have a driver drop a cargo chariot off at the guard station. Thank you."

"Right away." He disconnected the dolly from her chair and rolled it next to the elevator.

"Looks like you thought this through," Zuri said with a hint of exasperation in her voice.

"That's not even the half of it."

No doubt, Zuri thought. "By the way, how did you get those crates filled?"

Martina smiled with a look of pride and satisfaction when she said, “Your parents worked with the engineers to design this place totally for my use. I can access any crate and cart it anywhere within the vault. They used some of their future—”

Martina did not finish the sentence when she realized she was about to say too much. Instead, she said, “Never mind. You’ll find out soon enough.”

But she had said enough for Zuri to realize there was much more to her parents’ story than she ever imagined.

Chapter 16

When Martina stopped herself from finishing what she was about to say, she piqued her great-granddaughter's curiosity. Now, more than ever, Zuri wanted to dig into her parents' journals.

What was Gran about to say? Did she mean their future plans? Something they were putting off doing until the future? Future what? Zuri wondered.

Her parents told her they were not from Progensha and had come from the Great Beyond, but neither ever told her anything more.

Were they protecting me from something? Someone? she wondered.

She thought if they held things back from her, there had to be a reason. Now she wanted more than ever to uncover buried secrets. The urge gnawed at her. She devised the beginning of a plan.

Instead of schlepping herself and Pyperlyn back and forth to the vault, she decided to borrow a page from Martina's playbook.

"Gran?"

"Yes,"

"Are there any more empty crates available?"

"Lots."

"Mind if I fill a couple with my parents' journals and take them with me?"

Martina thought about it for a brief moment then said, "Sure." She looked at T'yree and asked, "How about you? I suppose you want in on this."

"You are correct, Lady—"

"What did I say about calling me that?"

"Apologies." He did his best to look contrite.

She looked at both of them before she sighed and said, “Alright, follow me.”

Zuri synced her pad to the internal surveillance system so she could keep an eye on Pyperlyn and followed her great-grandmother into the vault’s stacks.

Martina stopped at a section that housed crates of various sizes and told Zuri and T’yree to grab whatever they wanted. Then she led them to the shelves containing information relevant to their area of interest so they could pick whatever archival material they wanted.

T’yree chose things having to do with the early sols of Traveler City and before. Zuri picked whatever her crate would carry of things by her parents. She had to go back and get more crates. Zuri cleared the shelves of everything her parents recorded.

Satisfied with what they pulled from the shelves, they loaded the crates onto the elevator and rode it up to the guard house. A silver off-road pickup with a spacious cargo area was parked near the entrance. One of the guards helped load the crates into it while Martina held Pyperlyn on her lap and supervised. Once the crates were securely stowed into the cargo hold of the chariot, the family got inside and T’yree drove them home.

T’yree pulled into the driveway and offloaded the crates onto the dollies and rolled them into the house. He placed Martina’s in her bedroom, and theirs in an alcove off of the main room. Despite the roominess of their home, there was just too much to store in their bedroom. He and his wife agreed to set up a couple of workstations in the main room.

Chapter 17

The next sol, Zuri woke to the smell of something T'yree cooked for morning refreshment. Her stomach growled, giving her incentive to get up. She planned to eat, tend to Pyperlyn, then use the rest of her leave to begin learning things about her parents. She trudged off to the bathroom to get her sol started.

A loud burp from Pyperlyn greeted Zuri as she walked into the front room.

"Sounds like morning refreshment was delicious."

"As always," T'yree said. He put their daughter down in an infant chair, looked his wife up and down, then said, "Nice of you to join us. I was beginning to wonder if you were going to skip morning meal."

"I'm on leave. I'm not getting up early if I don't have to, but I'm not going to spend all sol lounging either. If I did, I would miss spending quality time with two of my favorite people."

She planted a soft kiss on her daughter's forehead and another on T'yree's. She sat down, said a silent prayer of thanks, then sliced into the food on her plate and swallowed a fork-full. It tasted like she bit into something from the Goddess's banquet table. Zuri closed her eyes and savored every nuanced flavor.

While she scooped, cut, sliced, and swallowed, they talked about their plans for the sol and for the rest of her maternity leave.

"It's my intention to dig as deeply as I can into my parents' records and learn more about them. It's bittersweet seeing them as they were back then. So alive and full of life. You can see the love they had for each other." She let out an exasperated sigh. "I miss them dearly."

"They would be very proud of you."

"You think so?"

"I know so. I am proud of you."

"Why?"

Without any hesitation he said, “You are an excellent wife and mother. You are a dedicated soldier and a successful engineer.” He glanced toward Martina’s room, lowered his voice and said, “And you are the only person who can put up with your great-grandmother.”

“That much is true.”

“I wish I had more time to go over the archives I gathered,” he said, “but duty calls. I have a full itinerary for the next few sols. I have many committees to oversee, dedications to attend, and disputes to settle. The work of a royal never ends.”

“Good thing you’re not a figurehead.”

“Why do you say that?”

“Because you would just be in everyone’s way.” She winked at him. “Now go make your royal rounds before you become a royal pain. I can finish up here.”

T’yree kissed Zuri and Pyperlyn then headed out the door.

Zuri mapped out her sol in her mind then gathered the dishes and placed them in the kitchen sanitizer. She returned to the front room and powered on her workstation and began viewing her parents’ journals. She picked up where she left off.

Chapter 18

While Zuri watched her parents' video recordings, Martina finished compiling the data she had worked on the night before as she ate the morning meal T'yree brought to her room before Zuri had gotten up. She scrutinized the information she pulled together from the crates in her room and decided it was just enough for what she had planned. Satisfied she had all of the information that would be needed, Martina composed a private coded message. It read: *Urgent. Have crucial information you will need. Get to my place as soon as you receive this message.* She clicked send and waited.

Two mos later, there was a knock at the door. Zuri paused her viewing, checked the security feed and saw Der'von standing at the door. *What in the Goddess's name is he doing here?* she wondered. She glanced at Pyperlyn, who was sleeping peacefully, got up and opened the door.

He greeted her with a nod and what passed as a genuine smile for him.

"Lady Zuri. Apologies for knocking, but the door chime does not appear to be functioning."

"Oh, yeah. Been meaning to get that fixed."

She gestured for him to come in. He wiped his feet on the mat outside the door before he crossed the threshold. He towered over her as he stood next to her. He had to be a head taller than T'yree.

Zuri closed the door, looked up at him and asked, "Councilman Der'von. What brings you to this part of the world?"

"Lady Martina. She messaged me and said it was urgent."

Zuri wondered what could be so urgent for a councilperson to show up at their front doorstep.

"Take a seat. I will get her."

"There is no need. I will receive him now," Martina said.

She had wheeled herself out to the front room when she heard the knock at the door. Her greeting was wrapped in guarded caution.

"Councilman."

He matched her caution with his own cool response.

"Lady Martina."

Despite the scorching Progenshan temperature, Zuri felt a slight chill in the air between her great-grandmother and Der'von. It was the fallout from their unresolved encounter the last time they debated, no doubt.

Martina attempted to warm that chill by acknowledging her part in the heated exchanges during their last council session.

It was not an apology, but it went a long way to mitigating his annoyance with her. He relented.

"Good. Now that the amenities are out of the way, I ask that you follow me to my quarters. What we need to discuss is of grave importance." She looked at Zuri and added, "And private." She looked back at Der'von and said, "Follow me." Then she whirled her chair around and rolled toward her room.

Der'von bowed respectfully to Zuri, excused himself, and fell in behind Martina. A moment later, she heard the distinctive snick as the lock to her door engaged.

Despite the enormity of the room, Der'von stood in awe at the sheer volume of archival material packed in it.

"Okay," he began, "what is so urgent?"

"As you may recall at our last meeting I said I had resources you would find useful."

"Yes, I recall."

"You are about to find out what they are. I suggest you sit down. What I am about to reveal to you will seem incredulous. I assure you that what you will see and hear is the absolute truth. And the magnitude of its implications will far exceed anything you can imagine. But before I begin, I will require one thing from you."

Here it comes, he thought. "And that would be?"

"That you swear to keep what you are about to learn between us—for now."

He wondered what could be so important that he had to swear to keep it secret. After giving it some thought, he agreed to her terms.

For most Progenshans, swearing an oath was a serious matter. If you swore an oath then broke it, you not only dishonored yourself, but you dishonored your entire clan and your ancestors. It was something one did not take lightly.

He crossed his arms in the Uderran manner of respect and said, "I swear on the honor of my forefathers that what I learn here this sol will remain between us."

Martina returned the gesture as a sign indicating she trusted his oath, then said, "Good. Now let us begin. Take a seat."

Chapter 19

Three mos into their meeting and Martina and Der'von were still in her great-grandmother's room. Martina had soundproofed it when the house was built, so there was no way for Zuri to know what was happening. They had either killed each other or they were deep in the throes of a secret, torrid love affair. Zuri cringed at the thought.

Now that's an image I wish I could forget.

Der'von never seemed to be a particularly cruel or violent man. Passionate about matters of civic and political importance? Yes. Violent? No. But Martina did have the propensity to bring suppressed traits to the surface. Zuri decided to wait and give it another mos before overriding the security protocols and bursting in.

However, neither scenario was taking place. The atmosphere in Martina's quarters was neither tense nor relaxed. It was closer to being impassive and neutral.

Martina began by opening up to Der'von about her childhood. She recounted everything she could remember right up to their heated exchange in council chambers. She tied all of that together by giving him a detailed history of the Travelers, who they were, and where they really came from.

How much she told him and what she told him depended on the vibes she got from him. Her empathic abilities allowed her to read him like a book. She could sense whether he was being persuaded or not. The more she revealed, the less skeptical he became.

Martina explained how the early Travelers had come from the Great Beyond. Of how their arrival was a tragic accident, and how they crashed in the Fertile Valley on what they called a starship named the *Michael P Anderson.*

"There is no place called the Fertile Valley," Der'von said.

"We know it as the Land of No Return." Martina paused long enough to allow what she said to germinate in his mind. "Damage to their ship released lethal amounts of radiation into the atmosphere resulting in the contamination of the air, land, flora, and fauna. They had no way of containing it. The higher lifeforms quickly died while the lower ones mutated," she told him.

"Those who survived the crash sought refuge far away from the radiation zone," she said. "Their trek took them to the Great Plains where they met the people who lived there. They told the Plains People they came from lands far away beyond all known boundaries, and that a disaster of some kind destroyed their homes and chased them from their land. They asked for permission to settle in the area. Fearful and distrustful at first, the Plains People were afraid that whatever befell the strangers might happen to them, but seeing the desperation of the strangers, they relented and let them settle in the area."

Martina could sense Der'von's mind calculating and his emotions churning as he did his best to understand and process the information she revealed.

"In the beginning, a few brave individuals, curious about the newcomers, ventured into the crash zone. They got sick and succumbed to their illnesses. A lucky few returned with tales of seeing a large craft buried in the ground, but they also died from exposure to the radiation. Others, curious about what they heard, foolishly searched for this amazing craft, but as the mutations took hold, they fell victim to the creatures that lived there. None returned."

Martina paused long enough to take a few sips of water before she continued.

"Many of the Plains People began to distrust the newcomers and agitated for their expulsion from the valley. However, cooler heads prevailed, and since the strangers kept to themselves and seemed to pose no immediate threat, they were allowed to stay."

Initially, Der'von found Martina's story about people from the Great Beyond hard to believe. He wanted to dismiss it as a scary tale you told young children, but she showed him irrefutable evidence about things regarding his own people that only the elders and a few select leaders of his clan had knowledge of.

"How do you know these things?" he asked.

"Let me show you," she said. And then followed up with video evidence and certified documentation. He discovered things about his own family that were unknown to him, Martina mentioned things no one outside of his family knew—or should have known. By the fourth mos, she had won him over. There was just one last thing she needed to reveal: the truth about what really happened to the valley.

She faltered when she began to talk about it. A few tears found their way down her cheeks.

Der'von was surprised to see Martina so distraught. He had never seen her as anything but headstrong and fearless. Seeing this side of her disarmed him. She quickly regained her composure and resumed telling her story.

"The destruction of the valley was not done by Thourons," she said. She sniffled and wiped her nose with a tissue. She had his undivided attention. Martina hesitated again before she said, "I am the reason the land and people were destroyed."

The revelation left Der'von speechless for a moment. He wasn't sure if he had heard her correctly.

"What do you mean you are the reason?"

"There was a powerful weapon that was aboard the crashed starship that I harbored in my house."

Still not sure whether to believe her or not, he asked, "How is it that you had this weapon in your possession?"

"Because I am the granddaughter of the *Michael Anderson*'s captain. I was entrusted with safeguarding it when I came of age."

He started to ask a question but did not know how to phrase it. "How ...?" Der'von let the word hang by itself in the air.

"The weapon was from the future," Martina said. "From another plane of existence. And it was not sanctioned by the government my ancestors came from. They fabricated a story that they were commissioned to build and test it."

She could sense his doubt. So she asked, "Didn't you stop to question whether the Thourons—or anyone else for that matter—had the technological capability to produce such a weapon?"

"No. I just assumed it was something new they developed and used against us."

"Think about it. They were on the verge of gaining access to scientific and technological knowledge that would have given them the tactical advantage. If they had gotten control of that information there would have been no way to stop them from using it against us. Why would they fight so long and hard to capture Traveler City only to destroy it and half the continent on the eve of victory?"

He had not considered that.

“So why are you the reason everything was blown to the Underworld?” he asked.

“We did not understand the destructive potential of the weapon. Its full power was unknown to us.”

“We? Us?”

She sighed. “Yes, us. Me, Lord T’iang, and Zuri’s parents.”

“The queen’s brother, Lady Lin and Lord Piper?”

“Yes.”

Martina sensed that Der’von believed her, but he was full of questions.

“So how is it that you and Lord T’iang are here, but Lady Zuri’s parents are not?”

“Because of what I failed to do. In a moment of weakness, I let them talk me out of doing what I was sworn to do.”

Intrigued and perturbed, Der’von made his first demand. “Explain how you’re alive and they are not.” He liked and respected Zuri’s parents and was devastated when they died. Now he wanted to know why and how.

“The weapon could only be activated manually and within close proximity to the detonator. I had every intention to remain behind and set it off so the Thourons would not get their murderous hands on it.”

Martina’s hatred of the Thourons was evident in her voice. Der’von wisely said nothing and allowed her to continue to explain.

“Lin and Piper were upset with me when I said I would not leave my home. Lin actually threatened to have me forcibly removed for my safety. When it became clear she meant to follow through with her threat, I told them about the bomb. T’iang suggested we take it to Uderra, but I insisted transporting it increased the chance of the Thourons intercepting it.”

Der'von was perceptive enough to know what Martina was about to say next. And said it before she did.

"So Lady Lin and Lord Piper stayed behind and detonated the bomb in your stead."

"Yes. They said since they weren't from Progensha, and because the bomb came from the time and place they were from, it should be them to do it."

That bit of news came as a total shock to Der'von.

"Because the bomb came from where they were from? Wait, are you saying that Lady Zuri's parents were not of this world?"

Martina looked at him with tear-soaked eyes and said, "Yes."

"If they come from the same place you say your grandfather came from, then how come they didn't live and die back then?"

"Because it was an accidental collision between the *Anderson* and their ship that resulted in the crash. But because of the time stream, they got pulled through and crashed later. Many cycles later. They were dragged through to our plane of existence two hundred cycles after the *Michael Anderson* crashed. They only arrived a little more than twenty cycles ago."

Chapter 20

Time streams. Other planes of existence. People and weapons from the future living in the past and present. It all made Der'von's head ache. When he recovered from Martina's revelation, he asked, "Does she know?"

Martina paused, sniffled, then dabbed her eyes with a tissue before she answered.

"No. She doesn't know. At least not yet."

"Not yet?"

"Correct. She is currently going through an archive of video recordings her parents left behind for her. I'm sure somewhere in them they tell her their true origins."

She stopped speaking and actually cried. She did not try to curb her tears. Der'von felt awkward as she openly wept. He was not prepared to see this side of such a strong-willed woman. When Martina regained emotional control of her senses, she said she was certain Zuri would hate her after she found out why and how her parents died.

Der'von tried to assure Martina that Zuri would find it in her heart to forgive her. Martina rejected the notion. Everything would change when Zuri found out they were not even blood related.

He attempted to assuage her concerns, but Martina could not be convinced otherwise. She was so certain of it that she took the precaution of securing a residence in the sector of the city Der'von lived in.

"I am fully anticipating being banished from the royal residence."

To Martina, it looked like Der'von's head might explode. What she told him was a lot to absorb. She sensed he still believed her. And she was not finished. But before he could toss a slew of platitudes her way, she continued to throw him off balance.

"Everything I have told you are things you should know. I have yet to tell you the things you need to know."

"There's more?"

"Yes. But I think you have heard and learned enough for now. I ask that you ponder what I have revealed to you. Once you have digested it, return to hear the rest—and bring Lolaan."

"Lolaan?"

"Yes."

Why?"

"Because she is as vital a part of the process as you."

"Process? What the drat are you talking about, and when did I become a part of it?"

"When you accepted my request to meet me here."

She picked up a small, slender case from off her workstation.

"Inside this case is a disc that explains everything she and you will need to know."

Martina handed it to Der'von.

"Tell her what I have told you, then give her this disc to view after you have had a chance to look at it. As a ranking council member and leader of her clan, it is imperative she also know what we know. And since the Exodus has already begun, the information I have may be crucial to all of you."

Martina alluded to a number of the smaller clans that had already begun leaving Uderra for parts unknown in the southern territories. They were deliberately avoiding the destruction zone by giving it a wide berth.

She heaved a heavy sigh and looked hard at Der'von as if her gaze could penetrate his soul.

"In a way, all of us have our futures already carved out for us. The Goddess has seen to that?"

"What do you mean? How are our futures already carved for us? The future is unknown."

"You still believe that after what you've seen?"

He had to admit that in this particular instance, some of the future was known. "But what—"

Martina waved a dismissive hand and told him she was too tired to continue and for him to leave.

"It has been a long sol. View the disc. Share it and what you know with Lolaan, then return at your earliest convenience with her."

She scooped up additional discs and urged him to take them.

"Here, give these to Lolaan after you have looked at them. It'll corroborate what I have told you so far."

"What are they?"

"Personal log entries. That's all I'm saying."

She pressed a button on the arm of her wheelchair and the room door lock disengaged with a whispered snick.

Taking that as a sign they were done, Der'von silently rose from his chair and headed out the door. He expected to see Zuri, but she was not in the room. A wave of relief washed over him. He did not want the added guilt of seeing her knowing he was privy to personal information she was not yet aware of.

Der'von let himself out of the house and headed for his chariot. He sat behind the wheel and tried to make better sense of what he had just learned. Before starting the engine, he keyed in a secure code on his wrist unit and sent Lolaan a message that said for her to meet him at his residence as soon as possible.

Lolaan sat in her council chamber office discussing evacuation plans with her aide Tameen. Like her, his Felid traits dominated. They were in the process of wrapping up their meeting when her wrist unit vibrated. She glanced down and saw it displayed an urgent message from Der'von. Her mind immediately went to thinking something was wrong. He wanted to see her pronto at his home.

The request was highly unusual because emergency meetings were always held in council chambers. She thought something must be seriously wrong.

She cut her meeting short and told her aide what she wanted the rest of her staff to do.

"Something just came up. Complete what you can and take the rest of the sol off. We shall convene at a later time to finalize the exodus strategy. Tell everyone they're free to do whatever they want once this is done."

A smile broad enough to reveal his white incisors spread across his calico face.

He replied enthusiastically, "Yes, Madam. I'll inform the others. Thank you." He got up, nearly trotted to the office door, and softly closed it behind him.

That's gotta be a record, she thought.

Mildly irritated at being interrupted as the pieces to the evacuation plan were falling into place, Lolaan looked at the clock on the wall. It was getting late. She had planned to finish up with the preliminary work with her staff then head home to a quiet evening of contemplative meditation. But it looked like those plans would have to wait.

She had a very capable staff. They were all ambitious and eager to please. Lolaan trusted them to get the job done without her guidance.

Alone and curious about what Der'von wanted to tell her, Lolaan keyed in a message to him on her wrist unit and said she was leaving and would be at his place within the mos.

Chapter 21

Forty mictons later, she drove up to his house and parked in the guest lot. Der'von was waiting for her at the front door. He let her in and got right to business.

"I have something of great importance to tell you and show you."

"It had better be. I gave up the rest of my sol to be here."

"Believe me. It will be worth it."

Der'von led her through an anteroom and into his private study. He gestured for her to sit at a personal computer workstation with display discs sitting next to it. The ones Martina had given him.

"Before we begin, you must swear an oath on your ancestors not to tell anyone what you are about to learn. I must inform you that only one other knows about what you are about to see and hear. "

"Who?"

"Swear the oath first."

Working with and debating Lolaan on the Uderran Council, Der'von had come to know her as someone he could trust, and as a person who personified integrity. If she swore an oath, she would be bound to honor it. He trusted the rest of his colleagues as far as believing they would stab him in the back and blame one of the others without a second thought.

Lolaan squinted at him with incredulous eyes before relenting.

"I swear on the memory of my ancestors to reveal to no one what I am about to learn." She continued to look at him with skepticism before she repeated her query, "Who?"

"Lady Martina. It was she who told me and gave me the data discs."

Lolaan remained silent for a moment before she asked, "Does this have anything to do with what she said at our last council meeting?"

"Yes."

Lolaan referenced a cryptic comment Martina made when she said she had resources that could assist them. At the time, she had dismissed them as an emotional display of bluster on Lady Martina's part in the heat of the moment, but surmised she was now about to find out how much was political posturing.

Der'von activated a soundproof shield around the room then launched into a detailed explanation about what she was about to see and hear before he booted up the workstation.

He dove into a straightforward explanation of what he could remember. He was brief.

Lolaan was not sure whether to believe him or not. Much of what he told her seemed like outlandish fairy tales. She would make a final determination once she saw what was on the discs.

Der'von sat quietly and patiently in a chair across the room while Lolaan scanned the data. He watched her facial expressions change from skeptical to astonished to disbelief to belief to acceptance.

Lolaan watched mesmerized until the end of the presentation. She looked at Der'von for several moments before she finally spoke.

"This is incredible. This means that everything we know—been told—is a lie."

"Pretty much."

"We are descendants of beings from the Great Beyond."

"Yes."

"Lady Lin and Lord Piper also came from the Great Beyond."

"Yes."

"Our ancestors and Lady Zuri's parents didn't just come from the Great Beyond, they also came from our future, and from a totally different plane of existence?"

"Yes."

“Does she know?”

“Some. Not all. Yet.”

“Yet?”

“Yes. Martina gave her discs her parents recorded through the cycles and bequeathed to her. She will eventually find out from them the truth about her parents and what they did.”

“The revelation of this knowledge changes everything.”

“There’s more.”

“More? What more could there possibly be after this?”

He held out a disc he had in his hand and said, “Look at this before drawing any conclusions.”

She took the disc he offered her and inserted it into the workstation. An image of Lord Piper and Lady Lin appeared on the screen. They had subdued expressions on their faces. Seeing them produced a feeling of sadness, but the feeling quickly dissipated when everything she saw and heard next stunned her. Lolaan’s heart skipped a beat when the two people on the screen addressed her and Der’von.

Chapter 22

Greetings Lord Der'von and Lady Lolaan. If you are viewing this, then that means we have joined the ancestors, Lin said.

Martina has no doubt explained to you the circumstances of our deaths. If she has not, ask her to tell you.

We asked Martina to give this recording to you because we recently learned what she has already told you and what she will tell you. She is a woman of her word.

Piper picked up the conversation.

Our only regret is that we will not be there when our daughter learns of what you will soon know. His eyes watered and he sniffled as he spoke. He paused before continuing. *Zuri will no doubt be very angry with us and with Martina. We ask that you intercede on our behalf when that happens.*

We know our daughter, Lin chimed in.

She used that comment as a segue to what she said next.

Right now you're both wondering how you're involved. Both of you have the strength of will, the wisdom, and the fortitude to follow through with what Martina will reveal to you. We have watched you both grow and mature into competent leaders. We believe you are the right people at what will be a critical time in our history to steer our people toward their destiny.

Piper spoke up when it looked like Lin was about to break down.

We could think of no others to trust with this information, he said. *We apologize for placing such a heavy responsibility on your shoulders. We're not asking that you commit, but that you at least consider what we ask.*

Lin, calm and composed again, picked up the conversation from there.

Martina is in possession of information no one in Uderra has or knows about. We ask that if you choose to do what she will ask of you, that you do so discreetly and wisely. We urge you … no, beseech you to at least give serious thought to taking on this mantle of responsibility because the future of Progensha depends on it. But if you decline, we … she will think no less of you. The choice is yours.

The screen went blank. The room was so quiet that Lolaan thought Der'von could hear her thoughts.

"I don't know if I should be honored or afraid," she finally said.

"The wise thing would be for us to be both."

"So what do we do now?"

"We meet with Lady Martina and find out what we need to know."

Lolaan checked the time on her wrist unit and saw they had crossed into the start of the next sol. There was no way she would be able to drive home, get adequate sleep, and be ready for work in time.

"I was supposed to meet with my staff later this sol to finalize plans for the exodus. Now it looks like I'll have to delay that meeting."

"Contact your people and tell them due to unforeseen circumstances you needed to confer with me about a pressing matter, and you will meet with them as soon as you can. I'll do the same with mine. In the meantime, you can sleep here. Then at dawns light, we will meet with Lady Martina."

After checking his security system, he disengaged the privacy shield and escorted her to the guest wing. They stopped at a spacious room tastefully decorated in neutral forest colors and adorned with artfully arranged flowers, a large double bed, modest workstation, and roomy bathroom. Next to the bed was a full-length nightgown and toiletries.

"I hope you find the accommodations to your liking."

He grinned.

Compared to her bungalow, this room was equivalent to a luxurious suite.

"The accommodations are more than adequate. Thank you."

"Good. I am pleased. When you are sufficiently rested, let me know and we will meet with Lady Martina. I will inform my house staff you are my guest for the duration of your stay here."

He nodded in a gesture of respect then left her alone in the room.

After freshening up in the bathroom, she curled up on the bed under a thick blanket and hoped she would be able to go to sleep.

Chapter 23

Sometime during the night, Lolaan had kicked the blanket from off the bed. She had not slept soundly. The information she saw on the discs occupied her thoughts. She was also eager and apprehensive to find out what Lady Martina felt was so important to pass along. She sat at the center of the bed engaged in morning meditation.

The light buzz of her wrist unit diverted her thoughts. A quick glance told her Der'von was calling. She clicked it on, but was not the first to speak.

"Good morning," he said. "I hope I didn't wake you."

All she could see was his face. He looked like he had a rough night. Disheveled hair and dark circles under his eyes. She could tell he was speaking into a desktop monitor because there was greater detail to his features.

"Good morning to you too," she said. "You did not. I was meditating."

She could see a skeptical expression find its way to his face. It was quickly replaced with an inscrutable smile instead.

"Good. Then can I assume you are awake enough to have a morning meal with me?" His smile became softer and more genuine.

"Yes, you may."

Der'von glanced down at his wrist then asked, "Shall I come to escort you in, say, thirty mictons?"

"I will be ready and waiting."

His smile broadened. It made his normally sullen gray complexion seem a bit warmer, her a bit uncertain. "I will see you then," he said.

Lolaan did not know why, but that brief exchange filled her with conflicted feelings. She had what her Terran brethren called butterflies in her stomach. Then from out of nowhere a lascivious thought invaded her mind. She quashed it quickly. It was a weird feeling. She returned to sitting in the lotus position until it was time for her to leave the room.

When the chime sounded, Lolaan looked at her wrist and saw that only fifteen mictons had passed. Der'von was early. She uncrossed her legs, slid off the bed and answered the door. A young woman with dark gray skin, wearing a pink flowing robe, bowed her head and offered a small package wrapped in brown paper. In a voice as soft as a whisper, she said, "Compliments of Lord Der'von."

Lolaan took the package and thanked the woman who smiled and quickly hurried away.

The door closed and Lolaan walked to the bed and proceeded to open it. Inside was a fresh change of clothing similar to what she wore the sol before. She was moved by the gesture. Her conflicted feelings returned.

Lolaan made her way to the bathroom to groom and answer the call of nature. She changed into the clothing given to her, neatly folded her old clothing and put them in the box, then sat on the side of the bed and waited while she mentally sifted through the information from the night before.

The second time her door chimed, it was Der'von. He greeted her with a warm smile as he looked at her in the clothing he sent her.

"You look like you're ready to take on the sol," he said.

"And so do you," she said.

Instead of his customary gray robe with hood, he wore a modest ensemble of black slacks and a matching shirt that hugged his masculine physique. She never thought he could ever look so good.

They both gawked at each other before Der'von extended a hand and asked, "Shall we?"

She took his hand with one of hers and carried her box of clothes with the other.

"Leave the box," he said. "My staff will attend to its contents."

"Are you sure?"

"Yes."

She laid the box on the bed and let him lead her out the room.

He escorted her to a large dining area where kitchen staff waited to serve them their food. They sat across from each other at a table large enough to seat four people. He gestured to the staff to begin serving.

"I hope you don't mind, but I took the liberty of having my staff fix a few Felid delicacies."

Impressed, Lolaan said she appreciated the effort he and his people took to accommodate her on such short notice.

"Good. I'm pleased our efforts were not for naught," he said.

Der'von waited for Lolaan to bless her food before he began eating. She was amazed at his courtesy. This was not the man she was accustomed to seeing. She expected the firebrand councilperson who was imposing, combative, and intimidating on the chamber floor. What she witnessed was a man who seemed mild mannered and insightful.

They engaged in light conversation before they went to his study where they discussed the reason they were having a morning meal together before Der'von contacted Martina.

Despite it being quite early, Martina answered the call with a surly, "You're late."

Der'von and Lolaan looked at each other bewildered before returning their attention to Martina.

Lolaan began to say, "Lady—" She was interrupted by Martina.

"What do I keep saying about how to address me?"

Feeling dejected, Lolaan said with a bit of resignation in her tone, "Not to use the courtesy title when speaking to you outside of chambers."

Satisfied she had finally gotten through to them, Martina said, "Good. Now finish whatever you two were doing and get your backsides over here ASAP." The air was filled with silence after Martina clicked off.

Looking like a couple of scolded children, Lolaan sighed and said, "Well, I guess we better get over there. We'll take my chariot."

“Fine with me,” Der’von said.

Following a white-knuckled ride through several districts, Lolaan drove up to the royal residence and parked in the VIP lot. They were greeted at the door by Zuri.

In as sarcastic a tone she could muster, Zuri said, “Her majesty is in her quarters waiting for you. I suggest you don’t keep her waiting anymore than you have.” She pointed toward Martina’s room. The two guests quickly headed for the open door before it closed and locked behind them.

Zuri watched with bemused amusement as two of the toughest members of the council rushed into Martina’s room like a couple of obedient children. She wondered what it was her great-grandmother had on them. She figured she would find out soon enough.

Chapter 24

Martina welcomed her guests, curtly dispensed with the pleasantries, then gestured for them to sit. They sat. She got right to the point.

"Not all of the original Travelers settled in the Open Valley, and we Uderrans are not the only ones to survive its destruction," she said.

Neither Der'von nor Lolaan said a word. They looked at her with baffled expressions. As far as either knew, everyone who fled the Great Plains had either settled in Uderra or the valley. But since the area was obliterated, only Uderra remained. There was nowhere else. Martina could sense their feelings of expectancy and apprehension. She was about to add astonishment.

"As you recently discovered, there was more to our ancestors than has been passed down. They were survivors of a catastrophic event. And like them, so are we. And also like them, we will prevail. But it will not be done simply by scattering ourselves to the wayward winds."

"Then how will it be done?" Lolaan asked.

"By developing a clandestine network of trust, communication, and cooperation."

"Clandestine?" Der'von asked. He derisively laughed. "Good luck with that. Trust and cooperation?" Der'von asked. "Like that's ever going to happen," he scoffed. "Though we've lived in relative peace with each other since the founding of Uderra because we have a common enemy, and can agree that staying here is not strategically sound in light of recent events, I can hardly agree that trusting our council colleagues would be in our best interests."

"I concur," Lolaan said. "Given the right incentives, I am quite certain they would betray anyone who threatened their existence."

"Or were an obstruction to anything they stood to gain," Der'von added.

"Which is why we will not be including them in our network," Martina said.

"So what are you proposing?" Der'von asked. "That my clan and Lolaan's clan join together with who? You?"

"Yes."

"To do what?"

"To ensure that what happened to the valley never happens again."

"And just how are we supposed to do that?" Lolaan asked.

"By joining with me and the inhabitants of the Dark Woods and the Mountain of the Goddess."

Martina sensed the bewilderment Der'von and Lolaan felt only grow deeper.

She began to explain.

"Not all of the crash survivors reached the Great Plains. They decided to split up in the hope that if misfortune befell one group, another might continue to exist. Those who made it to the Great Plains did not know how they would be received; if they would be welcomed or attacked. Fortunately, as we all know, the Plains People welcomed them and provided assistance. They settled in the Open Valley and established what became known as Traveler City."

"What about the other groups?" Lolaan asked.

"There were two other groups. One chose to head into the mountains. They believed if they survived, the mountains would provide natural cover and be easily defensible. The other group chose the Dark Woods for similar reasons. The thick underbrush, abundance of trees, and extensive forest was the camouflage they sought."

"So you are saying there are descendants of the crash survivors living on the Mountain of the Goddess and in the Dark Woods as we speak?" Der'von asked.

"On the Mountain of the Goddess? No. In the Mountain? Yes."

"And the Dark Woods?"

"Not just in them, but all through them."

"I've been to the Dark Woods. I have never encountered anyone living there."

“That is because they are experts in the art of camouflage.”

Lolaan’s curiosity was piqued. “So how is it that these additional groups are not in our shared history?”

“For the safety of all involved, they safeguarded their existence from the Progenshans.”

“So if they separated themselves from each other, how is it you know of them?”

“They maintained secret lines of communication amongst themselves. And as I told you, I am the granddaughter of the captain of the *Michael P Anderson*. I was granted clearance to participate in the communication network. Unfortunately, I am the last living member of the original network tied to both groups. When I’m gone, there will only be one other linking us to the other groups. When they are gone, the link will be severed—unless you two agree to continue my work.”

Der’von asked if it would be okay if he and Lolaan could discuss matters in the far corner of Martina’s quarters. She agreed to let them talk things over. The two huddled together and talked in a low whisper for several mictons before coming to a consensus.

“We have decided to accept your offer.”

“Good. The first thing you must do is meet the leaders of the Mountain People and the Dark Woods. Give me a sol or two to set things up and I will let you know when and where to meet.”

Der’von and Lolaan agreed to wait until they heard from Martina before activating their exodus plans. As they left Martina’s quarters, they passed Zuri who was holding her daughter in her lap and studying her workstation. They said goodbye and walked toward Lolaan’s chariot. She drove Der’von home, then headed to her own. They instructed their respective staff to continue with the Uderran evacuation plans until further notice. While they waited to hear from Martina, they reviewed the discs they were given and considered what alternatives might present themselves. Three sols later, they were sent messages to rendezvous at Lookout Cove before the crack of sunlight.

Chapter 25

Der'von and Lolaan arrived at Lookout Cove just as the first streaks of orange appeared in the sky. They were surprised to see Martina waiting for them.

Der'von greeted her with a taunting question. "Do you ever sleep?"

Martina returned his greeting with a bit of sarcasm of her own. "If you didn't sleep so much, you would have been here on time." She looked at Lolaan, who wisely remained silent. Looking back at Der'von, Martina asked, "Are you ready to unlearn all that you have learned?"

Her young companions nodded with uncertainty.

"Good. Follow me."

The sky was bright enough to maneuver without the aid of a trenchlight. Martina expertly rolled herself around a far corner of the precipice, along which a small pile of strategically placed waist-high boulders served as a guardrail. A short slope led to an unobtrusive path and what appeared to be a dead end. Der'von had been to the Cove numerous times, and considered himself a rather observant person, but he never noticed the path before, and neither had Lolaan. As they stood behind her wondering why they had been led to a path that went nowhere, Martina casually reached up and pressed one hand against the side of the mountain wall and pushed. They heard what sounded like a slight hum before a small portion of the wall slid aside revealing a glass control panel. When Martina placed her hand against it, a larger part of the wall in front of her opened like a pocket door revealing a passageway.

Martina rolled through the entrance before sensing her young companions were not following her. She swiveled to face them and asked, "Are you coming or have you gotten cold feet?"

After exchanging a befuddled look with each other, they crossed the threshold. When they did, the outer wall closed behind them with a barely perceptible hum. They stood in a claustrophobic passage, which barely accommodated the three of them that went nowhere. It was lit by a single, dim overhead recessed light. Martina rotated her chair to face a blank wall then placed her hand against that. It silently slid aside revealing a waiting elevator. This time, neither of her escorts hesitated when she rolled her chair inside. The door closed and the elevator abruptly dropped leaving them with the feeling their stomachs and other internal organs were still in the chamber above them.

“You could have warned us about the descent,” Lolaan struggled to say.

“You could’ve warned us that any of this was even here,” Der’von said, as he fought the urge to hurl everything he had eaten earlier.

A devious grin spread across Martina’s face before she asked, “Now where would be the fun in that?”

The elevator took them straight down for mectars before it changed direction and continued its descent on an angle further into the mountain’s depths until it came to an abrupt halt.

“We have arrived,” Martina announced.

The door slid open revealing a massive cavern filled with botanical gardens, running water, a tropical temperature, and people. Lots of people. It was almost like being in Uderra or Traveler City but underground deep inside a mountain.

They were greeted by a male, who looked to be around Martina’s age. He had grayish brown skin, smooth bald head, and green eyes. He wore a black hooded robe and was flanked by two much younger individuals. One looked distinctly Selemite with the obligatory grey complexion and black eyes. The other was a female who looked mostly Uderran with deep mahogany skin and aquatic features. Der’von surmised they were bodyguards. The older man bowed and spoke first.

“Greetings, Martina. You are looking well.”

“As are you.”

She introduced Der’von and Lolaan and said, “These are the two Uderran council people I told you about.”

“I am Kazi,” he said. “Welcome to Second Chance Mountain.”

“Thank you for inviting us,” Lolaan said. “Please forgive our ignorance, but why do you call it Second Chance Mountain?”

Kazi's mouth curved into a smile. "Because the ancestors who settled here said they were given a second chance at life." He looked at Martina then said, "Come. Follow me."

He turned and led them away from the elevator. The two guards fell into step behind them. They approached a waiting vehicle that resembled a chariot that floated on a cushion of air a half meter above the ground. He gestured for them to get in. The two escorts stood on platforms at the back of the vehicle and braced themselves against supports that rose up from the bumper. After they were settled, Kazi motioned to the driver, a young male, who appeared to be a full Uderran, to drive.

Following a short, smooth ride, they arrived at what Kazi called the Town Hall.

They exited the vehicle and walked through an enormous foyer carved from the surrounding rock. They came to a door at the far side. The two escorts stopped at the door and took positions on either side of it. Kazi ushered Martina, Der'von, and Lolaan in, then closed the door.

The room was furnished with various plants, animal skins, and highly technical-looking equipment.

"Welcome to my office," he said. "Please, have a seat. We have much to discuss."

Chapter 26

Kazi began the meeting by telling Der'von and Lolaan that he was briefed on what Martina had revealed to them, and that he and everyone living in the mountain were aware that the Uderrans and the Travelers were ignorant of the existence of those who lived inside the mountain.

"It was done by design," he said. "Our ancestors, who survived the crash, sought refuge far from the *Michael P Anderson.* The radiation exposure wasn't immediate, but inevitable because the containment fields were in danger of collapse. The survivors had time to evacuate and organize before full exposure. Our ancestors' prevailing thought at the time was to protect themselves without appearing to threaten the native peoples. And like your people are doing now, they divided themselves into groups and set out for parts unknown."

"To ensure that someone might survive and carry on," Lolaan said.

"Correct."

"One group headed for the mountains, one headed to the Grassy Plains, and a third headed toward the Dark Woods."

"Who determined who went with who?" Der'von asked.

"At first it was proposed to draw lots, but doing so would have divided families. Friendships would have been torn apart, and command hierarchy would have collapsed. The crash had done enough of that already. Ultimately, it was left up to personal choice. Of course, the hope was that those culturally, racially, and ethnically related would remain together, but the fear that an entire group could be wiped out by an unknown threat or disease led to the decision to leave it up to each individual to decide for themselves."

"Apparently, they were successful," Der'von said.

"Yes. There were those who were too injured or sick to make the trek. They remained behind or dropped out along the way."

"The nomads," Lolaan said.

"Yes, again," Kazi said. "Your ancestors were the ones who encountered the Plains People and the Hill People. Eventually, establishing Traveler City. My ancestors moved to the mountain, and the remaining group settled in the Dark Woods.

Lolaan, who was now sitting attentively on the edge of her chair, asked, "What happened? Why didn't you stay in touch?"

"We did, initially. But those who settled on the Plains decided to insulate the indigenous peoples from any more incursions. And when the Hill People became combative, and warlike, the Travelers broke off communication rather than risk escalating hostilities and involving us and those who settled in the Dark Woods."

Der'von refused to accept that the Travelers would simply cut off all communication. "There's just no way the Travelers would have terminated all communication with the other groups."

Kazi smiled then said, "Not totally, no." He looked at Martina before he continued. "As Martina here has told you, she is the last in a line of what we call Communicators."

Martina, who had remained silent, spoke up.

"Initially, the first Communicators were the surviving senior officers. As the war dragged on, and the communications equipment rescued from the *Michael Anderson* began to break down, replacement parts became scarce. What we could fabricate did not have the strength or range to maintain the efficiency necessary to keep the network viable. Alternative methods and rudimentary codes were devised to help maintain some measure of contact."

Martina paused for a moment of reflection. No one spoke while she took the time to gather her thoughts. Everyone could sense she struggled with uncomfortable memories. She eventually reconciled her recollections and resumed speaking.

"The attacks on the city grew exponentially and so did the casualties. The number of Communicators dwindled rapidly until only I remained. When I was injured by a terrorist attack, Lin and Piper stepped up to fill in as Communicators. They continued in that role until … their sacrifice."

She looked briefly at Kazi and saw his demeanor had taken on a solemn, melancholy nature. He started to speak but faltered. Martina continued speaking.

“As I told you, the survivors who became the Travelers were also the guardians of the sonic bomb that devastated the Plains. As a descendant of the captain, the responsibility fell to me to protect it, but as the Thourons threatened to overrun the city, I planned to stay behind and trigger it. But when Lin and Piper threatened to physically remove me from my home, I revealed the bomb’s existence to them.”

Kazi, recovered from his moment of weakness, interceded for Martina.

“And because of their sacrifice, we all stand here this sol. They bought us time to evacuate nearly everyone from the valley. Those who stayed behind bought time for the rest of us.”

“As a result,” Martina said, “I have been able to continue to be the liaison for Kazi’s clan and those of the Dark Woods. But I grow old and my time grows short. That is why, at the behest of Lin and Piper, I have chosen you both as my successors.”

“Why us?” Lolaan asked.

Kazi looked at them with eyes that seemed to penetrate their souls.

“We believe that you both have the wisdom, patience, fortitude of will, and the strength of character to lead your people and ours into uncertain times,” he said.

“We know that hard times are ahead,” Martina said. “We also know that Uderra will survive—or is supposed to—for the next three hundred cycles, but it won’t be easy.”

Der’von and Lolaan both appeared surprised.

Martina admonished them. “Don’t give me that innocent look. You’ve seen the records. You know where Lin and Piper came from. What you and we don’t know is what happens to the rest of us. And did what happened in the valley change the course of the future?”

“You see,” Kazi began. “Our fate and those of the Dark Woods is unknown because Lady Lin and Lord Piper were not privy to that information. What is known is that their time in Uderra’s future was short. What we also know is Uderra will still be at war with the Thourons. What we need to do is ensure that the future Lin and Piper knew still happens.”

Kazi and Martina began a tag team explanation with Martina sliding back into the conversation.

"With the destruction of the vale, the Thourons will be obsessed with getting revenge—on anyone. They experienced the largest loss of life in the glen. They will be motivated by revenge to exact retribution."

"But it was they who started this conflict," Lolaan protested.

"And it will be they who will continue it," Kazi said. "All those leaving Uderra will be targeted and quite possibly attacked. They will not wait to dress their wounds, assess the situation, or recover from their losses. They will strike back and strike back hard."

Der'von said, "The prevailing belief is the Thourons will exact revenge on Uderra. Which is the driving force behind the exodus."

Martina made no effort to mask the anger in her voice when she said, "Which is why we need to do everything we can to minimize any loss of life. Because there will be. Running from Uderra will escalate it, not minimize it."

"The Plains People are a proud and honorable nation," Kazi said.

"And stubborn," Martina added.

"And stubborn," Kazi agreed. "They will defend themselves and those leaving at all costs. That is why we must assist them. We must come out of hiding and make our presence known. We must let the Thourons know that they will not be fighting just the Uderrans and the survivors of Traveler City."

"But doing so will put your people at risk," Lolaan said.

"They are aware," Kazi said. "but it is time for us to join our brethren and shoulder more of the burden. For two hundred cycles, we have existed within the relative safety of the mountains."

"I hope you realize your offer to help may be rebuffed once the Uderrans discover you withheld your support for so long," Lolaan said.

"We are prepared to deal with the consequences."

“And I believe I may have the solution to mitigate that possibility,” Martina said. She did not elaborate.

“What do you need us to do?” Der’von asked.

“For a start,” Kazi said, “let the Uderrans know we will be sending emissaries.”

“We will need to contact our people and let them know there will be a change in plans regarding the exodus,” Lolaan said.

“Understood. I will take you to our communications center so you can contact your people. Your wrist units will not work this deep inside the mountain.”

Chapter 27

Tameen was awakened by the soft buzz of his wrist unit as it rested on the headboard of his bed. He groped for it until he had it in his paw before he opened his eyes. He looked at the readout and saw that it was Lolaan. He hurriedly smoothed back his hair before he answered. There was no way he was going to look less than ready in front of his boss.

“Greetings to you, Lady—”

Lolaan interrupted his greeting.

“Sorry to bother you so early, I need you to do me a favor. It is of grave importance.”

Tameen saw Lolaan was serious. Her normally pleasant appearance seemed off. She smiled, but it did not reach her eyes. He was wide awake and alert.

“Is there a problem?” he asked.

“No, there’s no problem, but something has come up. And I’m going to need your help.”

“Whatever you need, I will provide.”

“Good. For now, I just need you to stay on the line.”

“Will do, my Lady.”

His thoughts raced in his mind. He wondered what was going on. He began thinking of worst case scenarios.

While Tameen waited, Der’von’s trusted assistant had already begun her morning routine.

Talia, a creature of habit, was up and planning the sol’s agenda. She noted that her boss, normally an early riser, had gotten up earlier than normal and had left the compound without indicating why or where. It was unlike him to do either without notifying her. She hoped everything was alright. Her concern was magnified when her wrist unit buzzed, and she saw it was Der'von.

She answered with, "Are you alright, sir?" Talia scrutinized his features trying to tell if he was under stress or duress. He smiled.

"I'm fine. I just need you to hang on the line. You're being looped into a conference call."

An instant later, she was looking at herself, Der'von, Lolaan, Tameen, who had surprise and worry written on his calico features, and someone she did not recognize.

The face of a man who looked part Uderran and part Selemite dominated the screen.

"I am Kazi," the man said. "It is good to finally meet you. I have heard much about both of you. All good of course." He smiled broadly.

It was obvious that neither Talia nor Tameen were prepared. Both appeared to have the same perplexed expression of surprise.

"Permit me to explain," Der'von said. "Lord Kazi here—"

"Just Kazi. There's no need to be formal with me."

Der'von hesitated before he continued speaking. "Uh, Kazi here is offering to help us with our exodus."

"Pardon my asking, Lord Der'von," Talia began, "but who is this Kazi?"

"My question exactly," Tameen chimed in. "What is going on?"

"Much that will surprise you," Lolaan said. "Both of you."

"Look," Der'von said, "we can't explain it to you now. Meet us at Lookout Cove as soon as you can. We'll explain things after you get here. I suggest you come together. See you when you get here."

The screen went blank.

Talia and Tameen immediately called each other. Talia's call reached Tameen first.

“That was odd,” she said.

“Indeed,” he replied.

“Do you think they are in trouble?”

Tameen pondered the question before answering. “That was not my impression, but the whole thing reeks like swamp gas.”

“I agree. How about we meet at the council chambers and head out from there?”

“Sounds like a plan. I suggest we arm ourselves just in case.”

“Combat gear?” Talia asked.

“If there is indeed nothing wrong, suiting up in full gear may be excessive. But it might not hurt to go lightly armed.”

“What if it is a trap?”

“Then we will discover if we are meant to be martyrs or victims.”

“Neither prospect is comforting,” Talia lamented. “I will meet you as soon as I can. See you then.”

As soon as Tameen clicked off, Talia left a message with the compound’s security department that she would be meeting Tameen, Der’von, and Lolaan at Lookout Cove on urgent business. There was no way she was leaving without letting someone know where she was going. If she were to meet her demise, her family would not be left wondering why she was not still at the compound.

Talia finished her administrative tasks and then made her way back to her quarters. She exchanged her flowing gown for more practical street wear. Her choice of attire consisted of a workout tank top, gaucho pants, a pair of stylish knee-high boots with a low heel, and a loose jacket that stopped at her waist. The entire ensemble was black. She accessorized with a couple of holstered pocket pistols that fit nicely beneath her jacket. She selected an elegant dagger with an ornate handle made of hardened wood custom made for her grip that she could flick out from her sleeve on command.

Talia looked herself over in her mirror and made minor adjustments until she was satisfied with her appearance. She made one last check of her weapons then headed to her chariot parked in the underground garage and drove to the council chambers.

When she arrived, Tameen was waiting for her in the parking lot. He saw how similarly dressed they were. He wore a pair of camouflage combat boots with matching pants tucked into them. His shirt matched his pants and boots. Instead of a short jacket, he had chosen a long black duster coat that stopped at his knees. His tail swung freely unimpeded through a split in the back.

"And to think I thought I might be overdressed," he said.

"Great minds think alike," Talia said. "Shall we go see what surprises await us?"

"I thought you'd never ask. I'll drive."

"Fine by me."

Where Talia's chariot was a common street-rated model, Tameen's was more rugged. It was rated for the street, but was built primarily for off-road driving.

They rode a short distance to a checkpoint at an unfinished portion of the wall being constructed around the city. The guards were informed by Der'von and Lolaan that their assistants would be requesting passage to Lookout Cove. One of them checked the duo's credentials then waved them on.

By the time they reached Lookout Cove, the orange glow of the sky was bright enough to clearly see the rocky surface of the mountain range. They climbed the path to the meeting point where Der'von and Lolaan were waiting for them.

"Took you long enough," Der'von said.

"We got here as quickly as we could," Talia said.

"Considering the strangeness of the situation, I would think you'd be impressed with how swiftly we responded," Tameen said.

Der'von smiled and said, "Relax. I'm just having a bit of fun with you. You've done great. Now follow us."

Der'von and Lolaan led them to the hidden path. Tameen abruptly stopped walking, causing Talia to walk into him. She was about to complain when she saw what stopped him. Martina sat in her chair in what looked like a dead end. They both bowed in greeting and said simultaneously, "Lady Martina."

Martina returned their greeting with the nod of her head then said, "We are not in chambers. Drop the Lady and just call me Martina. Now follow me."

The young aides had the same thought: *Where?* They watched as she placed her hand on the mountain wall and were surprised when a glass panel revealed itself. They were further amazed as part of the wall slid open when she touched the panel. Neither of them saw how amused Der'von and Lolaan were watching their aides try to take in what they saw.

They stepped into a tight passage and were surprised to see the door to an elevator appear when Martina touched the wall. Almost as soon as they all piled into the cab the door closed behind them and it unexpectedly dropped down the shaft as if in freefall. Talia yelped and Tameen braced himself against the wall and blurted, "Drat!"

By the time they were able to compose themselves, the elevator stopped, and Kazi and his two guards were standing in the doorway. Instinctively, Tameen and Talia reached for their weapons, but Kazi's guards beat them to the draw and had their staves pointed at them. After a moment of hesitation, they raised their arms in surrender.

"There's no need for your weapons," Kazi said. "We're all friends here."

"By the Goddess," Martina said, "stop fooling around and follow me."

Kazi stepped aside as Martina rolled off the elevator, followed by Der'von and Lolaan. With their arms still held up in surrender, Tameen and Talia looked at each other then at the guards before they stepped off the elevator and into a world neither could have ever imagined.

"So that there are no, uh, misunderstandings," Kazi said, "I must insist that you surrender your weapons during your stay with us. I assure you, you are in good hands."

After they received silent approval from Der'von and Lolaan, the two aides produced their weapons and turned them over to the male guard while the female scanned them with a handheld device. Satisfied they were disarmed, she nodded to her partner who gave the guns and knives to Der'von and Lolaan.

Mildly amused, Kazi said, “Now that we have settled that pesky little business, I suggest we catch up to Martina before she leaves us standing here.”

By the time they reached Martina, she had already been helped into the waiting transport. They piled into the hover’s passenger cabin and were whisked off to wherever their hosts were taking them.

Talia leaned toward her boss and softly said, “It would have been nice if you had given us a heads-up.”

“Now what fun would that have been.” He grinned at both of them.

Lolaan chimed in, “You haven’t seen anything yet.”

Chapter 28

The little group rode in silence as the hover passed magnificent buildings, a slew of trees, water features, and people of every hue and variety. Kazi let his guests absorb as much as they were able. He could see they were awestruck. A quick glance at Martina assured him she was as entertained as he was with their guests' reactions. The unguided tour eventually came to a stop outside an enormous building.

"We have arrived," Kazi announced. The two escorts flanked Kazi and Martina while the rest of them stepped out of the vehicle. The little group found themselves standing in front of what appeared to be a great hall carved into the mountain. Its architectural design made it look like it was a natural formation within the rock structure. Kazi led them inside while the escorts took up positions on either side of the enormous doors leading into the lobby of the hall. It looked like a giant planetarium. "This sol will be an education none of you have ever experienced."

"And full of unexpected surprises," Martina said. "Beginning with this one." She looked at Kazi who simply nodded.

Lolaan and Talia gasped as Martina stood up from her wheelchair and walked. Tameen and Der'von just stared, mouths open, in shock.

Anticipating their questions, she simply said, "Nanites."

Lolaan recovered from her astonishment first and asked, "Nanites?"

Martina smiled and said, "We call them micro healers."

"Martina had nanites injected into her system following a major battle during one of the sieges of Traveler City," Kazi said.

"During that siege," Martina began, "many defenders were administered nanites to repair wounds. Lin, Piper, and I were among those who received the first generation of living nanites. Unfortunately, their injuries were more severe than mine, so they became the first to receive permanent, living nanites."

Der'von, the next to regain his wits, asked, "Wait, you have been able to walk all this time?"

The question was asked as if the entire explanation of nanites never happened.

“Not until recently.”

“How recent is ‘recently?’”

“Within the last quarter cycle.”

“And you thought to withhold this bit of information because?”

“Because,” Kazi said. “We and the nanites have only been able to repair and restore people with standard injuries.”

“You *and* the nanites?” Talia asked. Finally, over her initial shock.

“Yes, they are sentient.”

Tameen, the last to recover from the bombshell revelation, asked, “What do you mean by sentient? I thought they were micro machines that repaired injuries then were expelled by the body or surgically extracted.”

“In the beginning they were, but as the science progressed, so did the nanites.”

“Lady Lin and Lord Piper were the recipients of the first generation of permanent sentient nanites,” Martina said.

Our scientists and physicians began collaborating on developing more advanced nanites once they saw how Lady Lin and Lord Piper benefitted from them.

“They are just one of the many things we can assist with if you are willing to let us,” Kazi said with an air of enthusiasm. “But first, you must learn what your bosses have already learned. Unlike them, though, your experience will be more … immersive.”
He gestured toward the many seats around them.

“Please, take a seat and enjoy the show.” The playful humor in his delivery was subtle.

Images, still and moving, began to play on the walls and ceiling all around them. It was an audiovisual documentary experience of the history of Progensha. The narrators were Kazi and Martina.

Five mos later, what started as a graphic portrayal of the inception of Progensha ended with images of the destruction of the valley and the departure of those choosing to leave Uderra in real time.

Though Der'von and Lolaan did not learn much new from the presentation, they were impressed with the multimedia display. Seeing a visual representation served to reinforce their understanding and clarify a few uncertainties.

For Talia and Tameen, the illustration solicited a visceral feeling of historical knowledge that ingrained itself into their very souls. But they each harbored doubt as to the validity of what they saw.

"How can we be certain what we just witnessed is historical fact and not a theatrical display fabricated for our benefit to persuade us to stray from our course?" Tameen asked. His expression was simultaneously curious and suspicious.

Talia was equally as doubtful. "Yes," she agreed. "How can we be certain this is not some elaborate ploy to dissuade us from our plans?"

Martina stood up and addressed them both with a slightly annoyed tone in her voice.

"Because I have lived much of the last one hundred cycles. I am a living witness to a large portion of Progensha's recent history. I am the last living descendant who personally knew those who crashed over two hundred *years* ago. I was a child when the last survivors were still alive."

She made it a point to emphasize her use of the word years instead of cycles to illustrate her heritage. Native Progenshans said cycle, as the word year was never a part of their languages or vocabulary. Martina continued to make her point by noting that natural Progenshan speech patterns were more formal and they did not use contractions or truncate their words. The descendants of those from Traveler City and those of mixed heritage often did. She noted the differences in speech among everyone in the room.

Once she was done lecturing, she walked over to Tameen and Talia and stood within their personal space before she continued.

"You are well within your rights to doubt or disbelieve what you just learned. If you choose to continue believing what you learned growing up, that is your right. Neither I nor anyone else will further attempt to dissuade you. But before you solidify your beliefs, I ask that you consider one more thing."

Martina paused, then motioned to the escorts by waving for them to either come in or let someone in. The relative darkness of the room, in conjunction with the light that beamed in from outside, obscured the identity of the person who entered. As they came closer, both Tameen and Talia became visibly flustered. Dumbfounded, they reverently bowed, and clumsily crossed their arms across their chests when they saw who it was that walked toward them. Talia spoke first.

"Greetings, My Lord."

Tameen echoed the greeting with the same level of reverence.

The newcomer stood next to Martina and returned the greeting. He flashed a broad smile then said, "Relax yourselves. There is no need for you to heighten your levels of discomfort on my behalf."

The young aides lowered their arms and stood gobsmacked looking at T'iang. The brother to the Uderran queen.

He winked at Martina and nodded toward Kazi before speaking to Tameen and Talia again.

"I understand there is a lot for you to take in," he said. "By the time this is over, all of this will become clearer. But before we begin, permit me to introduce our final member."

He turned and motioned to the guards to let someone else into the room. The latest arrival was covered in a brown hooded robe, and appeared to glide rather than walk down the dark room giving the impression of someone with grace and importance. The mysterious figure stopped and stood next to T'iang and Martina before removing their hood. The stranger who revealed themselves was the most striking individual either of them had ever seen. She was a beautiful amalgam of exotic beauty.

It was like the Goddess gave her the best genes of her lineage. Her skin was an unblemished chocolate brown with a slight tint of gray, her button nose was framed by thin, barely visible whiskers. Her yellow eyes and pointed, cupped ears were feline in appearance. A pair of antennae adorned the top of her head which was crowned by a complimentary blend of red, brown, and white hair. Although the robe covered much of her body, the unmistakable outline of a muscular, toned physique was hard to ignore.

The nails and fingers on her hands looked both elegant and lethal. When she smiled, a strikingly impressive pair of perfectly white incisors accompanied it. Her feet were covered in severely polished black boots resembling those worn by Terran swashbucklers in ancient times.

“Greetings,” she said. “I am Siren. Ruler of the Dark Woods Clan.”

Her voice was a whispered purr laced with a hint of assured command strength and a touch of playfulness.

Der’von and Tameen gawked without saying a word. Lolaan and Talia stared absolutely awestruck. None of them said anything, but questions swirled in their heads.

Martina and T’iang were amused at the astonished reactions of the others and decided to let their young charges goggle a few awkward moments more before Kazi took control of things.

“Good. Now that we’re all together, let us begin. The first thing I suggest is contacting your people to assure them you are all well. This confab may take a few sols. In the meantime, I recommend we take a nature respite and refresh ourselves before we begin.”

He tapped a button on a small hand-held device he pulled from a pocket and motioned to a couple of guards who entered the room. He pointed toward Der’von, Lolaan, and their aides.

“Take our guests to the communications center so they may contact their people and inform them of their wellbeing.”

The guards nodded and gestured for the four Uderrans to follow.

While the rest of the attendees availed themselves of the facilities, a catering staff brought in food and drinks. They set everything up buffet style on tables adjacent to where the group was convening.

Everyone made a concerted effort to keep the conversation light and not talk business until Der’von and company returned, and Kazi determined when the break was over.

“Let us resume our discussions,” he began.

They all took their seats and continued where they had left off.

“In light of what happened in the valley, my people have concluded our seclusion is no longer a prudent position to maintain,” Kazi said.

“Agreed,” Siren said. “Mine as well. Our self-imposed isolation, in hindsight, has left us all vulnerable. We will take a more active role in this conflict and no longer allow our brethren to shoulder the burden alone. But we will not expose ourselves to undue danger as our Traveler City cousins did.”

Martina protested in a brusque tone.

“I disagree with your assessment. We did not expose ourselves to any undue danger. We were the unfortunate victims of an organized campaign by violent bigots who sought our removal and enslavement. We simply chose to resist.”

Siren reverently bowed and extended her arms in a gesture of surrender. She said, “My apologies, Martina. I did not intend to insult you or your ancestors.”

Regretting the bluntness of her response, Martina returned the gesture and said, “Apologies. I overreacted.”

Kazi attempted to lower the tension in the room when he rubbed his hands together and said, “It’s good to see a bit of lively discord taking place. That means we’re all engaged. Does anyone wish to contribute to the current topic of discussion?”

Der’von stood up and directed his question to Siren.

“Just how do you propose to lend Uderra assistance while limiting your exposure?”

“It is the position of the Dark Woods Clan to expand our involvement with a support network of operatives who work in the shadows while continuing to shield our population from harm.”

“What do you mean, ‘expand?’ ‘Work in the shadows?’ How can you expand upon something that does not exist? I have been extensively through the Dark Woods. I never encountered anyone or anything that would remotely indicate an extensive populace—or inhabitants of any kind.”

Martina, Kazi, and T’iang exchanged glances before Siren calmly explained.

"Do I not exist? I saw how you and your colleagues looked at me. Am I a figment of your imagination or do I stimulate it?"

Taken aback by the question, and slightly chagrined, Der'von reluctantly said, "Neither."

Unphased by his reaction or response, Siren continued.

"Moments ago you thought the Dark Woods was uninhabited. It is not. My people live deep beyond the heart of the woods within the protection of an electronic camouflage net. Before this sol, only those we trusted knew we existed."

She nodded at Kazi, Martina, and T'iang then returned her full attention to Der'von, Lolaan, Talia, and Tameen.

"This sol, our presence has become known to others, but our whereabouts will remain shrouded in mystery. You see, there is a loose network of covert operatives from the Dark Woods, the Mountain of the Goddess, and Traveler City who have been working with … the Thouron resistance."

A quiet pall fell over the room before Der'von, Tameen, and Talia were instantly on their feet protesting in a crescendo of angry overlapping voices. Lolaan sat quietly stunned trying to decide how she felt about the situation.

Martina stood up from her chair and shouted above the others, "Shut Up and Sit Down!"

They fell silent, but did not sit. She glared at each one and demanded through gritted teeth, "Now!"

Once they did, Martina took a moment to gather her thoughts. When she had, she spoke in her normal tone of voice.

"As it is understandable that you would harbor and express such strong opinions about working with the Thourons, I do not disagree with them, but I can say with assured certainty that they are unfounded. Because there is already an established network of Thouron resistance operatives working with us. And have been for over one hundred cycles. Their number is small, and they suffer greatly when discovered, but they have remained steadfast in dedicating themselves to the cause."

Despite the room's size, there was a silence that made it seem small and claustrophobic. Lolaan was the first to break that silence with the quiet fortitude she was known for during council debates, "Surely, you cannot be serious."

Martina locked eyes with the young councilwoman and emitted a low guttural growl of disappointment. The impatience in her eyes was unmistakable. The frustration in her voice was restrained.

"Do I *look* like I'm joking?"

After a moment of quiet hesitation, Lolaan said, "No."

"Good. Because I find none of this humorous."

After composing herself, Martina continued speaking. "Our little alliance, if you will, has worked for the most part. No, it has not been easy keeping it secret. Yes, we have had betrayals, but the network has endured for cycles, and we have instituted safeguards to ensure that it continues."

When no one raised any objections, posed questions or challenges, she said, "Now prepare yourselves for another revelation of greater importance."

With all eyes focused on Martina, no one but Siren and T'iang saw Kazi gesture to the guards to let another person in the room.

As soon as the doors opened, a figure walked in, made their way down the aisle, then stopped next to Martina. Everyone but Kazi, T'iang, and Siren was dumbstruck. Standing before them was a female Thouron. No one moved or said a word. The tension in the air seemed thick enough to asphyxiate the room's occupants.

Kazi cut through it by nodding at the latest arrival and said, "Introduce yourself."

The pale-skinned visitor crossed her arms and bowed in the Uderran manner of showing respect then said, "Esteemed leaders, my name is Andorra, and it is my most sincere wish to work with you in your struggle against my people."

Chapter 29

After several sols of sitting on committees, overseeing the settlement of disputes, and performing other expected royal duties, his itinerary was finally clear. T'yree looked forward to relaxing once he arrived home. He had tried to contact his father on several occasions to consult with him on a few things, but he was not able to reach him. When he asked his aunt about T'iang's whereabouts, she said his father was busy working on something important and did not wish to be disturbed. She refused to elaborate. He thought it was out of character for his father to remain elusive and was almost willing to take his aunt's reticence at face value, but he thought it was rather odd that Lady Martina was also incognito. But since it was not unusual for her to disappear sols at a time, he did not give much weight to his misgivings. He nearly dismissed them until word began to spread that Der'von, Lolaan, and their personal assistants were unreachable. Their staff would only say they were away on urgent business.

He put his suspicions aside as he pulled into the driveway and turned off the low hum of the engine. Seeing his wife and daughter would alleviate some of his concerns. Out of habit, he surveyed the area around the house before he got out of the vehicle and walked through the front door. He half expected to see Zuri waiting for him, but it was late. Even his always-on-guard spouse needed downtime.

He peeked in on his ladies. Both appeared to be asleep. He was certain Pyperlyn was sleeping but suspected Zuri was listening in her sleep. Even though she was a member of the Uderran Corps of Engineers and not a combat unit, he could never forget her parents were battle-hardened soldiers. Their teachings and her military training were ingrained. Once a soldier, always a soldier.

T'yree backed out of the bedroom, glanced at the closed door to Martina's room, then strolled into the kitchen to fix himself a light late evening snack. Despite a sol full of meetings, dedications, speech appearances, and luncheons, he was not tired. So he decided he would use some of his downtime and continue viewing the data discs. He thought they might make him drowsy and help him drift off to sleep.

It had the opposite effect. What he watched reinforced much of what he already knew, but energized his enthusiasm. The genesis of Progenshans is shrouded in mystery and early spiritual beliefs. The most commonly held convictions and teachings said that the Goddess traversed the Great Beyond until She came upon Progensha. Deeming the planet welcoming, rich in abundant resources, and worthy, the Goddess gave birth to the planet's many children. She taught them what they could understand, then sent them to the far territories to cultivate the land and procreate.

The Goddess created the massive ocean leviathans to protect her children from those of far away lands who turned away from her teachings and might do the faithful harm.

T'yree's ancestors, who became known as the Plains People, lived peaceful lives in harmony with the land, air, and inland seas. They were basically hunter-gatherers. They tilled the soil for crops, hunted the animals for food and clothing, and venerated the Goddess. Oral traditions eventually gave way to the written word.

There was a distinctive change in the narrative voice as summarized texts transitioned to testimonial writings.

Even before the written word, his people lived in virtual isolation for generations. As they came into contact with others, their societal dynamic changed accordingly. They traded occasionally with other tribal groups like the Hill People, who eventually became known as the Thourons, and various nomadic groups. Then the equilibrium of the planet was altered in one sol.

The slow, natural development of the Great Plains residents changed dramatically around two hundred cycles ago when a group of strange-looking people with even stranger ways suddenly appeared in need of assistance. Nearly two hundred individuals from various races appeared at the border of the Plains and asked for help.

Their hues ranged from charcoal to translucent. Some had smooth skin while others had scales or that of the texture of stone. Others had hair, fur, or tightly woven tentacles. Then there were those who had extra appendages, were missing noses, or had multiple eyes. They sent emissaries bearing unusual gifts in exchange for help.

The strangers said they had come from a far away land which experienced a disaster that resulted in the destruction of their homeland and the deaths of many of their people. They were searching for a place to resettle. They called themselves the Travelers.

Initially skeptical and reluctant, the Plains People were frightened by these newcomers, their bizarre appearances, and peculiar ways. If they had come from lands beyond anything the Plains People knew, how was it they survived the leviathans? According to religious tradition, the Goddess had placed the leviathans in the Colossal Ocean to keep people from far away lands from reaching the Plains People. Some wondered how they had survived the journey. There were those who believed not all far away lands were separated by the ocean.

Yet, there were others who believed these strangers were the leviathans who somehow became land creatures and were out to devour everyone. A few even believed they were a lost tribe of the Goddess's children who had disobeyed her and were being punished as a result. But after much debate, the elders convinced everyone to help. By not helping, they would fall out of favor with the Goddess if they refused to aid her children—no matter where they came from or how bizarre they looked.

The Plains People cautiously assisted with resettling the Travelers in the Open Valley. A wilderness unsettled by anyone. The strangers proved themselves to be peaceful and sincere at their word. They appreciated the help and showed their gratitude by introducing T'yree's ancestors to new and innovative ways to farm the land, domesticate the animals, and fish the sea.

Along with teaching them new ways to harvest, the strangers showed the Plains People new and wonderful healing techniques and brought with them the knowledge of advanced science, engineering, and something they called technology. They did this all while respecting the traditions and sovereignty of his ancestors. Many of the strangers even adopted the ways of his people and assimilated into his culture. The end result was the development of a prosperous hub of trade and commerce.

What began as a modest settlement transformed rapidly into a town, then into a city. Over time the Travelers traded extensively with most of the indigenous tribes. In the beginning, even the Hill People traded with their new neighbors. But to the Hill People, the success of the Travelers was seen as a threat to their expansionist plans. They withdrew from everyone and secluded themselves in the hills.

Their self-imposed isolation incubated a seething jealousy that manifested into micro aggressions that escalated into outright hostility toward everyone else. The feared threat to the Plains People did not originate from beyond their borders, but from their neighbors adjacent to them.

It started with the Hill People damaging property or destroying crops in the dead of night, then progressed to raids and physical attacks on individuals and small groups until it escalated to night-rider-style violence. The aggression toward their former trading partners became a consolidated movement of outright hate. The Hill People coalesced into a supremacist society with a militaristic orientation. Their mindset was focused on establishing regional dominance at any cost.

At the outset, they were prone to fight each other as well as their neighbors until one leader reigned supreme. A bigoted despot called Neander Thouron. His followers, and eventually all the Hill People, adopted his name as their identity. His dominance was due in part to his ruthlessness and a blind allegiance by his more fervent followers. Neander's popularity was due in part to a cult of personality. He had a charismatic nature that appealed to the baser instincts of his followers. They had primitive urges that needed to be fulfilled. Neander skillfully satiated those needs.

The Thourons became skilled at organized violence and excelled at dispensing it. It was to their advantage that the Plains People and the nomadic tribes were peaceful. Only the Travelers proved more effective at keeping them in check.

T'yree's people and the nomads eventually got better at defending themselves. But as time progressed, it became increasingly difficult to guard against the ruthlessness of a determined enemy predisposed to violent conquest and subterfuge.

After nearly two hundred cycles, the Thourons had become much more than an irritating nuisance. They were an existential threat to everyone living in the Grassy Plains, Traveler City, and the surrounding territories. The plains residents had become targets of a regime focused on enslavement, genocide, and brutish conquest.

By the time Uderra was established, the conflicts had morphed into full scale war. If it had not been for the foresight of Lady Lin and Lord Piper, everyone living in Uderra might not currently exist.

T'yree was so absorbed in the information he viewed on the data discs that he did not realize how much time had passed. The first of Progensha's two suns made its presence known as it peaked over the mountains and brushed the morning sky with hues of peach and orange. It cast a sliver of light through the privacy shades at the window across the floor. The second sun soon followed.

Fortunately, he had nothing scheduled and had planned to spend the sol doing what he wanted and not what his position demanded. Even a royal needed some time off. T'yree was about to shut down the workstation when he thought he saw his name flash on the screen. He had blinked at the time and was not sure what he saw. So he rewound the player several more times and stared at the playback each time, but did not see his name flash before him. It seemed almost subliminal. Probably due to lack of sleep.

He decided to try something he thought was rather silly. He planned to blink at the moment he thought he saw his name. T'yree played back the video and blinked and saw nothing. It was a foolish action, but felt he had to try it. Then another thought formed in his mind; it should have been his first. Now he did feel foolish. T'yree replayed the final sectons of the video one frame at a time.

He painstakingly advanced the video frame by frame and was rewarded for his efforts. One frame had his name and a series of letters and numbers. He had not imagined it. *Could they be a code of some kind?*, he wondered.

He took a screenshot of the frame and transferred it to his wrist unit then advanced the video a few additional frames in case there was more to see. There was not. So he let the video play to the end and ejected the disc before he heard, "Morning, my love. You're up early."

T'yree nearly jumped out of his skin.

"Do not do that. That could have been the death of me."

Zuri flashed a devious smirk on her face as she entered the room with Pyperlyn propped on one hip.

"It'll take more than a startled greeting to be the cause of your demise," she said. The smirk transitioned into a quizzical stare before she said, "I know you didn't come to bed last evening. What was so captivating about the archival data?"

His heart, no longer pounding from surprise, T'yree told his wife that he had not felt tired when he arrived home so he checked on his ladies, fixed something to eat and became immersed in the files. He simply lost track of time.

"That must have been some interesting reading," Zuri said.

"It was!" His unbridled enthusiasm was palpable, almost childlike. "I have always been interested in our history. The data in the archives filled in gaps and answered a few questions."

"Did you find what you were looking for?"

"Yes. A better understanding of the origins of our people and the history between us and the Thourons. It is interesting how, as time passes, events in history become distorted or forgotten."

"By those who control the narrative."

"And others."

"Like the Thourons?"

"Yes."

Zuri was insistent. "But mostly the Thourons."

T'yree sighed and said, "Yes."

"And because of them, the valley became a target of conquering bigots of the underworld determined to subjugate and eradicate those not like them. Finally destroying half the continent in the process."

He acquiesced with a slight nod.

Zuri seemed intent on ignoring anything else her husband was trying to say. T'yree heaved another sigh and asked, "Did you know that at one time they were known as the Hill People, and our people traded freely with them?"

"Did you know our people were once known as the Plains People before they were forced from their ancestral lands by those same people?" The sarcasm was obvious.

It was obvious Zuri had no love for the Thourons. And the loss of her parents did nothing but deepen her hatred of them.

"It is curious you should say that because things took a negative turn two hundred cycles ago," he said. "When the Travelers arrived."

"Why would the appearance of the Travelers make a difference?"

At the risk of illustrating her point, he said in a lower tone, "Evidence suggests the Hill People had ambitions of gaining influence in the valley, but the Travelers hindered their plans. They viewed the newcomers as competitors at best, and as invaders at worst."

"I believe you meant to say dominance, not influence. I suspect they always had ulterior motives. Do the records say when they decided to exert their so-called influence?"

“Not precisely. The records do state that they withdrew and became isolationists. When they reemerged, they were calling themselves Thourons, and embarked on a campaign of aggression toward others. They have continued to do so ever since.”

“And all of that culminated sols ago with the destruction of the valley.”

Zuri was adamant about blaming the Thourons for the huge loss of life and the deaths of her parents. T’yree knew she would not rest until she got her revenge. Eager to change the subject, he asked his wife if she wanted him to fix her something to eat.

“I love how you spoil me, but I must learn to make my own food if I ever find myself starving to death and you’re not around. I will fix myself something and feed our daughter.”

“Then what?” he asked.

“Then I will resume viewing the archival records Martina gave me.” A dreamy expression found its way to her face. “It’s been kinda nice to see my parents again,” she said. Zuri made her way to the kitchen to fix food for herself and Pyperlyn.

Happy to see his wife smile a genuine heartfelt one since the first time she held Pyperlyn, T’yree said he was going to go to bed. He shut down his workstation, slipped the disc into his pocket, trudged to their room and flopped on the bed. He tossed and turned unable to go to sleep. The concealed message gnawed at him, taunted him. He reached for his laptop computer unit, which sat on a nightstand adjacent to his side of the bed, inserted the disc, and resumed scouring the archival data.

Chapter 30

Many sols came and went, and there was no word about the whereabouts of either T'iang or Martina. T'yree became increasingly concerned and tried every avenue he could think of to find out where his father might be. He even attempted to pry information from his aunt, but she would not answer his queries.

It had also been several sols since Der'von, Lolaan, and their assistants became unreachable. To compound his worries further, he had listened to the secret message Lady Lin and Lord Piper embedded in the disc that was part of the archival record he had obtained from Lady Martina. It had disturbed him.

They explained that they were from the Great Beyond, but were also from the future, and that their daughter knew where they were from, but not when. The final bit of information they revealed was the existence of a bomb from the future, and that Martina and his father were the only others who had knowledge of its existence. Lin and Piper said they stayed behind in Traveler City to ensure the Thourons did not get their hands on it. They lamented not being there for Zuri, and asked him to watch over their daughter. Before they signed off for the last time, they said they left a recording for Zuri revealing everything, and asked him to be there for her.

Following a rather trying sol filled with disappointment and frustration, T'yree sat on the edge of the bed and sulked. He continued to encounter roadblock after roadblock in his quest to find answers. It was beginning to grate on his nerves. Just as he was about to head off to the bathroom he heard a terrifying scream emanate from the front room followed by a crash.

His heart skipped a beat as he grabbed a pistol he kept fastened to the bottom of his nightstand. T'yree flipped off the gun's safety and raced to the front room to be confronted by a furious Zuri. She was pacing the room, cursing and tossing anything she could get her hands on. The only expression on her face could not be mistaken for anything but pure, unadulterated rage.

He flipped the safety back on and slipped the weapon into his waistband at the small of his back just as Zuri began muttering.

"Where the hell is she? Where the hell is that little virago?"

"What virago?" he asked.

Zuri whirled toward T'yree and hurled a disc in his direction. It whizzed past his head and bounced off the wall. He was certain she missed intentionally because she had an accurate throwing arm.

Not wanting to be a target anymore than he already was, T'yree summoned up the strength to make his voice sound as meek as he could then asked, "What are you talking about?"

"Don't play stupid. You know damn well who." She paused to take a breath before continuing. "She knew the truth this whole time and didn't say anything. And now she's conveniently missing."

"As is my father." He said it with cool indifference and without any inflection. His tone disarmed her. The revelation surprised her.

Zuri stopped speaking and pacing. She turned a concerned eye toward him before asking with a hardened edge to her voice, "When did he go missing and when were you going to tell me?"

Not sure how to answer, he simply said, "A few sols ago. I wanted to be certain nothing was amiss before mentioning it." Anticipating her next question, he said, "I already asked my aunt, and she is not talking. All she said was something important came up and he needed to tend to it. He left no clue as to where he went or why. No one else in the family knows what is happening."

"They don't know or they're not saying?"

"I do not know."

"I bet it has something to do with my great-grandmother. That woman can never leave well enough alone. She probably convinced him to do something foolish and now both their lives are in peril." Zuri stood wringing her hands and seething. "I swear, if she isn't already dead, I'm going to kill her when I see her."

Seeing the current situation as good a time as any, T'yree decided to ask, "Why are you so angry with Lady Martina?"

"Because of this."

Zuri snatched a disc from off her workstation and tossed it to her husband. He flinched expecting her to launch it at him. He caught it and looked at the label. It was addressed to Zuri from her parents. Without saying a word, he walked over to the workstation and inserted it. Moments later the images of Lin and Piper appeared. They both appeared haggard, living specters of how he remembered them. Lin spoke first.

Hi, Munchkin, by now you have gone through all of the discs we made for you. This one is our final message to you. It's been transmitted to Martina using her patented encryption algorithm. No one will be able to decipher it. And she has sworn to never open it. Lin displayed a sorrowful smile. There was no joy in her eyes.

We asked Martina to decrypt it and hold this one back until she felt the time was right to give it to you. The war for Traveler City is not going well. Unfortunately, we won't be able to leave and join up with you in Uderra. Lin's voice cracked and she faltered. Piper picked up the message.

Remember when we told you we were from the Great Beyond and not from Progensha? Well, there was one teeny tiny thing we didn't tell you. We're soldiers from the future, and from another universe. Uderrans refer to it as a plane of existence. We come from one of those planes three hundred cycles from now. Technically, we haven't been born yet.

He stopped to think about what he said then corrected himself.

Well, in our universe, we're still alive, but in this one, we haven't been born yet. While passing through a time portal, our ship collided with a science vessel that was passing through at the same time. That ship crashed on Progensha two hundred cycles ago. We got pulled through and crashed on Progensha about a cycle before you were born. We had no way of getting home and nearly died. Martina and T'iang rescued us and took us in. They are the only other people who know. By the time you see this, at least three others will also know.

He looked at Lin then took hold of her hand before he continued.

There's one more thing we need to tell you. The reason we have stayed in Traveler City is because there is a bomb in Martina's house. It's from the other ship. And it can only be set off by close proximity to the detonator. Martina was going to stay behind and destroy it, but we gave her no choice.

Lin's smile reappeared, but the fear in her eyes pulled at T'yree's emotions when she continued where Piper left off.

She wouldn't tell us why she was going to stay behind rather than evacuate until I, uh, sort of threatened to kick her ass and drag her back to Uderra. That's when she came clean. She is the granddaughter of the ship's captain and was entrusted with safeguarding the bomb. We told her since it was from our time, and we're somewhat responsible for it being here, it should be our responsibility to destroy, not hers. Do not blame her, Munchkin.

What we have chosen to do will be the most difficult thing we will ever do. We wish things could be different, but your survival, your very existence depends on what we have to do. We pray that you never feel the terror we feel right now. We hope some sol you can find it in your heart to forgive us.

After a moment's hesitation and a few sniffles, Lin said, *If there's anything to be gained from this, it's that the one constant in the universe is that nothing is constant.*

Following a brief pause, both Lin and Piper said together, *We love you, Munchkin.* Then the screen went blank.

T'yree looked up from the workstation to see tears streaming down Zuri's face like a waterfall. He reached out and pulled her toward him into a warm embrace. She rested a cheek on his chest and sobbed uncontrollably. As much as he wanted to assuage her discomfort, he felt he had no choice but to add to it.

"I have something I need to tell you," he said. He took a deep breath then said, "I'm one of the three others."

Fully expecting to become the target of a caustic tirade, T'yree was caught completely off guard when Zuri continued to sob in his arms. The light vibrations from her trembling coursed their way through his body. He continued to hold her waiting for the emotional tide to shift, but it never did. She simply asked him a question.

"When did you find out?"

"A few sols ago." He sighed. "Your parents left me a hidden message in one of the discs I was viewing. They said not to say anything until you had a chance to see the disc they left for you. I am sure this disc is the one."

She drew in a large breath then slowly exhaled. He wondered if she was attempting to calm herself or was drawing strength for another outburst. But she continued to calmly hold him without resorting to any aggressive movements. He kissed the top of her head and stared out into the room not focusing on anything in particular before he spoke again.

"You cannot blame Lady Martina anymore than you can blame your parents."

"I know," she sighed, "but it felt good to blame somebody."

"So what are we going to do now?"

She pulled slightly away from him, looked up into his eyes and said, "The first thing we're going to do is find out who the other two people are. Then we're going to find out what happened to your father and my great-grandmother."

Zuri and T'yree began their investigation by asking their queen about what she knew of her brother's disappearance. She remained stubbornly uncooperative, dismissive, and refused to discuss it. Her nephew thought it was due to being distraught. Zuri suspected something more was going on. Especially when no one else in the royal court would talk to them about it. Even the senior military officers were evasive. It all seemed so unlike the queen or her advisers to put a clamp on something so concerning. Compounding the issue were the disappearances of the others. Conspiracy theories began to surface.

As the sols came and went, the rumors gave way to one that was openly being discussed. People were convinced Thourons had somehow abducted Lord T'iang, Lady Martina, Lord Der'von, Lady Lolaan, and their assistants. It was widely believed the kidnappings, or possibly murders, were devised to keep the people fearful and concentrated within the walls of the city for some reason known only to their enemy. The disappearances served to reinforce the belief in some that leaving Uderra was the right move.

The Exodus took on a new urgency for the survivors of Traveler City and the valley. Only the former Great Plains People remained resolute. They were forced out of their ancestral lands once before; they were not going to be coerced into fleeing their current home. The Uderrans had invested too much to abandon it all now. They adopted the motto: "Live free or die free."

Chapter 31

As people fled in droves to what they presumed was safer territory, a lone individual watched it all unfold. Concealed in a formation of jagged boulders high among the cliffs that formed a natural physical boundary between Thouron territory and the former valley, Nadir watched the activities of those below. He was perched in his observation post overlooking a hideous scar on a land that once swarmed with life.

Although the valley no longer cradled life, life coursed along its perimeter as a steady arterial flow of people left Uderra for parts unknown. Initially, those leaving the city began as a trickle, but quickly grew to steady streams of evacuees like snaking fingers in all directions.

There were some who migrated to the inland seas. Others chose the regions along the Colossal Ocean or the Western Sea. A small contingent settled on the periphery of the Dark Woods. There were a few brave souls who traveled to the desert lands bordering the Land of No Return.

The general consensus was these stalwarts were gambling with their lives living so close to the mutations that roamed the land. Those who chose to live there believed they would be less inclined to be attacked because of their close proximity to the radiation barrier. They also did not intend to make their settlements permanent. Constantly meandering along the border meant they would always be on the move and present themselves as less desirable targets.

But no matter the reason or eventual destination, none dared travel through the destruction zone. Wherever they went, every emigrant gave the Rocky Hills a wide berth. They were all headed away from Thouron territory.

Securely tucked away in his hidden vantage point, Nadir pondered a nagging thought. No one was attacking Thourons. Not one of them was seeking revenge. Not even the Uderrans. What he observed were people fixated on getting as far away as possible from his people. He watched as survivors scattered like the winds to the far reaches of the continent. He imagined some would have sailed away to the farthest corners of the planet if it were not for the leviathans that lived in the Colossal Sea. He wondered if the Goddess created those monstrous creatures so Progenshans would eventually learn to coexist. After all, they did before his people flipped the script.

What he knew of Progenshan history was what he had been taught growing up. There had been no war or hostilities until the strangers arrived. All Thourons were taught that these strangers threatened the stability of the land and weakened its delicate balance. These strangers also threatened the security and sovereignty of the Thouron nation. Indeed, the very existence of the Thouron people. Their mere exoticness was considered an abomination in the eyes of the Goddess.

Nadir had accepted this doctrine without question until he became an intelligence officer and witnessed heinous atrocities committed against their so-called enemies. These acts of barbarism were what prompted him to begin to question the righteousness of the Thouron cause.

Was it not his people who were the abomination? Nadir believed his people's take on history and religion was suspect. Why should these people he was taught to hate be considered anything but brothers and sisters since they were all created by the Goddess? None of them had threatened his people in any way that he ever saw. They were always on the defensive, and here he was helping to wage war and exploit people who only wanted to be left alone and live in peace.

As he watched from his perch, he saw desperate people reluctant to abandon everything they knew, but willing to flee to parts unknown, toward an uncertain future, rather than become victimized by a relentless pursuer. Nadir questioned his part in it. He also wondered why there were not more Thourons like him who questioned their actions and motivations rather than blindly following the party line.

Nadir resigned himself to accept the realization that he lived under a brutal authoritarian government keen on squashing contrary beliefs and thoughts. His people willingly allowed themselves to be led by cruel men and women who sought by whatever means at their disposal to gain, maintain, and wield power over others. They perverted everything decent. What began to bother him was his participation in it.

He was preparing to break camp and relocate when something caught his attention. *Was that a flash of light?* he wondered. Movement within the devastation zone. At least he thought he saw movement. *Had someone survived*? he wondered. *Could it be that the destruction was not total?* Nadir focused his magnifiers on the area that caught his interest and studied it intently. However, he detected nothing out of the ordinary. Perhaps Andorra was correct. Maybe he was losing his judgement and his sanity.

As dusk descended over the area, he planned to grab a bite to eat then head out at dawn and set up camp at another point along the ridge to see what he could observe of those leaving Uderra.

He gobbled down some food ration packs, chased them with a couple swigs of water, then packed his gear for the move.

He swung his backpack over his shoulder and erased all evidence of his presence when another flash caught his attention in the waning sunlight. Nadir was certain he was not hallucinating. Determined to find out what it was he saw, he traversed the ridge to get as close as he could to the light source without being detected.

He was an expert tracker and could follow anyone or anything without revealing himself to his quarry—as well as evade anyone who might attempt to follow. Nadir calculated his route and estimated the time it would take to reach his destination. Then he took an energy bar from his pack and headed toward what he now called the heart of darkness.

Chapter 32

The group in Second Chance Mountain engaged in lively discussions that were at times cordial and other times tumultuous and downright combative. At the moment, they were neither. Kazi wisely suggested they all take a break for a few mos when Martina sensed they had reached an impasse. Everyone either took the time to clear their minds and calm down or they napped. Emotions had run hot. A cooling down time was needed.

At the height of their discourse, Der'von, backed by Tameen, vehemently opposed allowing Thourons into the inner circle. Martina and T'iang supported the opposite position. Lolaan did her best to keep things from exploding into chaos, and while Talia remained silent, her body language clearly telegraphed that she supported Der'von and Tameen. Kazi and Siren sat on the sidelines with Andorra who yearned to get involved since much of the vitriol was about her and directed toward her. She felt a nagging urge to defend herself in the face of all the hostility.

When she was finally fed up with being the target of their ire, Andorra stood and shouted, "Enough!"

Once she had gotten everyone's undivided attention, she walked to the center of the gathering and stood in silence for a moment. Andorra looked at Siren who appeared to nod her approval. She deliberately faced Der'von, Lolaan, Talia, and Tameen before she spoke again.

"It is clear that you despise me and my people. I get it. I truly do, but I will no longer sit here while you talk about me and my people as if I am not in the room. I am no longer like them, and have not been for cycles. We are all not the same."

"That still remains to be seen," Tameen said.

He had fully understood that Andorra meant all Thourons were not the same, but felt compelled to take a verbal jab.

Incensed that Andorra dared to speak and interrupt, Der'von challenged her.

"If you 'get it,' then you should know why we feel as we do. Hundreds, no, thousands of innocents have died by the hands of you people. How do you expect us to suddenly forget and forgive that? From where I stand, you're all the same."

Andorra glared at Der'von. The outrage clearly written on her face suddenly changed to something unreadable. To everyone's surprise, she slipped off her boots and then calmly unzipped the front of her uniform. She let it drop to her feet, stepped out of it, and stood before them completely naked. Her arms and hands were outstretched in a beseeching manner.

In a strong and steady, yet impassive voice, she challenged them with one statement.

"Do with me what you will. I am as you see me now. I am not what I was. Slay me with your words or with your weapons. I will not resist you; I have nothing left to hide, and nothing left to give but my life."

Andorra continued to stand before them in silence. Though she was unmistakably female, that femininity was muted by the grotesque scars that covered her body. Testaments to the life she lived as a soldier and spy. She made no effort to put her clothes back on.

She stood naked before the group and slowly rotated so no part of her body went unnoticed. She looked at every person in the room as they reacted to what she showed them.

It was obvious her nude form surprised her audience, but it was the scars that shocked or appalled them the most. Her intent was not to be prurient but to edify.

"The older scars are from my youth when I was naive and fought against your people as one indoctrinated by the teachings of my culture." Andorra's voice was strong and steady. She did not waver. "The newer ones are from fighting against my people." The inflection in her tone did not change.

She pointed to each repulsive welt and gash, and graphically explained how she got them. She displayed no humiliation for her nakedness. Only the shame of her actions as a pawn of a contemptible government and reprehensible culture was unmistakably apparent to all.

When she finished her impromptu demonstration, Andorra stood motionless with quiet defiance as some stared at her while others looked away. It was clear the exhibition made all of them uncomfortable. Siren was the first to fill the silence when she stood up, walked to Andorra, and placed an assuring hand on the woman's shoulder.

"You may put your clothes back on."

As Andorra dressed, Siren continued speaking.

"Yes, Andorra is a Thouron. And, yes, she fought against and killed many of your people, but she has killed many of her own as well. If her subterfuge is ever discovered, she will be made an example of."

Der'von started to ask a question.

"How can we know that she can be trusted to—"

Siren interrupted him.

"We don't. Anymore than my people can trust you and yours."

"But we have never waged war against you."

"Because you did not know we existed. Had you known, would you have not tried?"

"No! We are not aggressors."

The anger behind Der'von's words was palpable, and so was his earnestness.

"Can you speak for the rest of your brethren?"

He was about to say yes but stopped. There was a time when he would have said yes without hesitation, but recent events cast a pall over things now. He thought of the many times he disagreed with his council colleagues and the many battles he lost regarding what direction to take in their war with the Thourons.

"No," is what he said instead.

"And therein lies the dilemma. I understand how you feel about Andorra and her people. Believe me when I say I share your trepidations and concerns about them. But when it comes to her and her associates, I can attest to one thing. She, and they, are trustworthy and sincere in their desire to help. I owe my very life to them."

Siren stepped closer to the center of the room before she spoke again.

"Many years … cycles ago, while on a reconnaissance mission, I was captured, beaten, interrogated, raped, and slated for public termination. I was branded a filthy Traveler.

She grabbed the collar of her tunic and ripped it to reveal a literal brand on her chest. She let the shock of the reveal stew in their minds before she continued.

"I live with this reminder every sol. I cannot look into a mirror without seeing it. I cannot bathe without feeling it. I cannot make love to my partner without the knowledge that they see it burned into me and are reminded of what was done to me. The pain of its impression into my skin is indelibly ingrained into my memory. Your hatred of her people comes nowhere close to mine."

For a brief moment, the calm demeanor displayed by Siren threatened to crack, but she reigned in her emotions and remained in control.

"Andorra and her comrades liberated me on the eve of my execution. While her team created a diversion, she helped me escape. We were both badly wounded during the effort. We each nearly died from our wounds."

More curious than defiant, Der'von asked, "So how is it that you both found your way to this mountain when no one knew your people or the mountain people existed?"

"Our cohort."

"Cohort?"

"Allow me to interject here," Martina said.

Siren nodded her approval and walked back to her seat and sat next to a fully clothed Andorra.

"There were resistance cells working on the outskirts of Traveler City. As far as the Thourons knew, all of the resistance fighters were from there. The only people who knew the whole truth were Lin, Piper, and me. They were to succeed me when I passed beyond the veil. But … " Martina faltered before regaining her composure. "But when they perished instead, I was the sole point of contact and communication. If something was to happen to me, the line of communication would be broken. So I enlisted T'iang. He agreed to join me, but insisted we all become a more cohesive group. No one person should have to shoulder the burden and risk tearing asunder everything we built if they met their demise prematurely. That is why we are gathered here now."

T'iang stood and faced the group. Certain he had their undivided attention, he proceeded to speak.

"Besides Siren, no one here has more reason to hate the Thourons than I and Martina. She has lost five people she loved dearly. One of them was my wife, callously murdered by Andorra's people."

He paused to steady himself as thoughts of his wife crossed his mind. It was clearly obvious that her death still deeply affected him. Once he got over the emotional hurdle, he continued.

"For cycles, I harbored a deep hatred that festered in my heart. When Martina first came to me with her revelation and request, I outright rejected it. But after some praying to the Goddess for guidance, I decided to turn that hatred into something productive."

He turned to look at Siren and Andorra before he finished speaking.

"When Siren brought Andorra to me, my first instinct was to kill her where she stood, but I realized the short term satisfaction would not bring back my Sylvia. It was not easy, but I decided doing so would make me no better than those who killed my wife. I decided the best way to defeat our enemy was to do so from within."

"And that is when we chose to coordinate our efforts," Siren said. "Not just communicate through a liaison. That is why we are all gathered here this sol. Do you not agree that we would be stronger together than not?"

When no one responded, Siren stood, slipped out of her robe and asked, "Do you need to see my wounds as well?"

Almost immediately Der'von, Tameen, and Talia dissuaded her from further disrobing.

With what appeared to be a thaw in the deliberations, Kazi jumped in and called for a recess.

While everyone answered the call of nature and got something to eat or took naps, Kazi, Martina, and T'iang huddled together to discuss what had just transpired and to plan their next steps going forward. Andorra and Siren quietly left the planetarium together.

“It appears we have a long way to go before we reach some sort of accord,” T’iang said.

“We knew it would be an uphill struggle,” Kazi said, “But I believe we have made some progress.”

The three of them quietly discussed and debated their options and decisions. Occasionally taking breaks to eat or to relieve themselves.

“It will take them a while to come around,” Martina said. “Do not forget Der’von and Talia are primarily of Selemite heritage. The same as me. There is a stubborn streak buried deep within our lineage.”

“What if they do not come around?” Kazi asked.

“Then Lin, Piper, and myself have made a grievous error in judgment.”

“I do not believe you have,” T’iang said. “Remember, there are two more pieces to this puzzle that have not come into play as yet. I believe in my son’s ability to sway his wife to our cause.”

“And I know my great-granddaughter. She was well trained by her parents. Learning about them, my part in their deaths, and this tenuous alliance and the cycles it took to build–especially with Thouron operatives–may result in it all coming undone.”

“I pray that you are wrong,” Kazi said. “Or this could develop into a protracted conflict with no future or end.”

“We all know what future is destined for our planet,” Martina said. “We know that this damned war will continue on for another three hundred cycles. What we don’t know is how it will end. We owe it to Lin and Piper to at least try to ensure the future they knew comes to pass and plays itself out, or we do our best to make sure the worst does not happen.”

“And how do you propose we do this?”

“By using the blueprint Lin and Piper left behind. We will execute as much of it that we can, then destroy all evidence that we did.”

“I say it is time we get them involved,” T’iang said. “My sister has informed me that our absences are having widespread impact throughout Uderra. The rumors have accelerated as has the Exodus. People are saying we have been captured and possibly killed by Thourons."

"Then I say we move swiftly to assuage any concerns with the populace and do damage control," Martina said. "As for Zuri, I will endure whatever repudiation she deems upon me. Partial or total. But I will not let it interfere with the plan."

Kazi's communicator buzzed. A quick glance at it let him know Andorra and Siren had returned. He informed the group they were back. The two women entered the planetarium and rejoined their colleagues.

"Is it done?" Martina asked.

"Yes," Siren said.

"Do you think he saw it?"

"Yes."

"Do you think he'll come?"

"Yes."

"Do you think he will join us?"

"That remains to be seen."

"What if he doesn't?"

Andorra let go of a barely audible sigh filled with despair before she said, "Then he will die."

Chapter 33

After having been stonewalled for sols in their efforts to unveil the mystery behind the disappearances of T'iang and the others, Zuri and T'yree were summoned to report to the queen immediately. An armored chariot was dispatched to pick up the couple and their daughter from their compound and drive them through the sprawling complex to the palace.

They were met by members of the queen's royal guard and court nannies upon their arrival. The guards escorted Zuri and T'yree to the queen's chambers while the nannies were charged with caring for Pyperlyn.

T'yree's aunt was in a small sunroom tending to flowers in her private garden when the captain of the guard announced their arrival. She'ara turned to look at her guests as they entered the room. She was the spitting image of her brother, but with a feminine physique. Twins tended to run in the family. Her light green eyes appeared to see right through them. She turned back to her flowers, snipped one off a stem, cupped it in her hands and breathed in its fragrance.

Following protocol, Zuri and T'yree stood in silence waiting to be acknowledged and addressed.

She'ara put the flower in a vase on a table next to her and continued snipping as she spoke to them.

"I have asked you to come before me because I am now in a position to answer your questions about your father and the others."

She paused to prune a bush of purple flowers, increasing the anticipation of her audience, before she continued. Her demeanor was nonchalant. As if nothing was amiss. She did not look in their direction.

"Your father and the others have been … how shall I say this?" She paused and looked pensive for a moment. Thinking of the appropriate word. She settled on one and said, "Preoccupied."

"What do you mean 'preoccupied?'" T'yree asked. He intended to sound angry, but his question came across being more anxious.

"Busy. Working. Immersed in business of great importance," was her impartial reply.

“What kind of business could be so important that he, they, would leave the rest of us in emotional limbo?” Zuri asked. “Are they so insensitive to our feelings that they would ignore the burden of sorrow we all carry? And what about you, your Majesty, do you not care about your own brother?”

Her query was laced with an unmistakably indignant tone lurking just below the surface. She did not try to mask it. Queen or no queen, Zuri refused to be intimidated or have her concerns ignored.

She’ara did not whirl in anger toward Zuri’s disrespectful attitude as she expected her to. She slowly, deliberately turned to face her.

“I would mind your tone, young lady, lest you further cross the line of disrespecting your queen and run afoul of my patience and good graces.”

The rebuke was not uttered by She’ara. It was spoken by her brother. T’iang had come from a room adjacent to the sunroom. He stared hard at his daughter-in-law.

The threat was so full of restrained iciness that it was enough to send a shiver through Zuri. And that was difficult to do. She quickly bowed with sincere respect and apologized.

“Please forgive my impudence, my Lord.”

T’iang pierced her with a penetrating stare a moment more before his expression softened slightly.

She’ara returned to pruning as if Zuri’s irreverence and T’iang’s verbal warning never happened.

Stunned by what had just transpired, T’yree looked at his wife with both consternation and irritation manifested on his face before he found his voice. “Why all the subterfuge, father? Why was I, uh, we not kept informed?”

“Because we deemed it necessary to exclude you until you had an opportunity to peruse the archival records,” She’ara said.

“You knew?”

She turned and faced them. “Of course. I am the queen. Why would I not know?”

“You let me, us, believe something unfortunate had befallen father. We were worried.”

He turned to face T’iang.

“Rumors among the people have them believing you and the others met your demise at the hands of our enemy.”

A new voice entered the conversation from behind them.

“That couldn’t be helped.”

Zuri and T’yree turned and faced Martina sitting in her wheelchair. Zuri’s ire crescendoed.

“Why you conniving little—”

One word, sternly spoken with a jarring forcefulness by T’iang, stopped her in mid sentence.

“ENOUGH!”

There was not much that unnerved Zuri, but the utterance of one word by her father-in-law sent a chill through her soul. It felt like the Goddess had stepped aside and told T’iang She would not interfere.

“You seem to have forgotten that we value respect over impudence. If you are angry, you are entitled to your anger, but when it imprudently crosses the line and enters the realm of disrespect, you open yourself to punitive measures.”

He raised an eyebrow and asked, “Are you prepared to take a chance with that?”

Zuri did not have to think twice. Without hesitation she crossed her arms, bowed, and said with abject reverence, “Apologies. My Lord. My Queen. Great-grandmother.”

Twice in just a few mictons. Martina could sense Zuri’s emotions were all over the place. She had let control of them slip.

Seeing such a proud woman humbled this way, pulled at Martina's heart. But she knew they could not afford for things to disintegrate into an emotional quagmire. Her great-granddaughter would soon regain control.

"Accepted," She'ara said.

"Now that we have the childish frivolity out of the way," T'iang began, "I suggest we be on our way."

Zuri and T'yree exchanged a curious glance as Martina wheeled herself out the room and commanded, "Follow me."

Without hesitation, they fell into step behind her. Followed by T'iang. She'ara returned her full attention to her pruning.

They walked silently behind one of the guards as he pushed Martina's chair towards the armored vehicle. When they reached it, Zuri broke her silence.

In as even a tone as she could muster, asked, "Where are we going?" Then, as an afterthought, said, "If you do not mind me asking."

T'iang responded. "To meet with the others."

His tone was pleasant and conversational. It was as if the earlier tension between them never happened.

Not inclined to ask anymore questions, she resumed being quiescent and boarded the transport along with the others. They were driven through Uderra's main checkpoint and soon sped along the heavily guarded road to Lookout Cove.

Many of the visible fortifications along the route were a direct result of Martina's influence and Zuri's direction as the senior officer in the Uderran Corps of Engineers. The invisible ones were what she was most proud of.

When they arrived at the Cove, the guards escorted them to the precipice then positioned themselves within bunkers that were carved into the rock formations. Zuri wondered when they were built. She never signed off on their construction. She made a mental note to find out who authorized them. They continued to follow Martina down a path she had never seen before until they reached a solid wall at the end of it.

Zuri wondered if Martina was exhibiting an early stage of mental decline and thought, *Great, the old woman has brought us to a path to nowhere.*

She was about to say something snarky when Martina pressed a hand against the side of the mountain wall and pushed. There was a slight hum before a portion of the wall slid to one side. Behind the part of the wall that opened was a glass control panel. Martina placed her hand against that and a larger part of the wall slid open revealing a passageway.

Surprised at what she witnessed, Zuri uttered a phrase she had heard her parents say whenever something caught them off guard. "What the hell?"

Martina rolled into a small passage that also appeared to lead nowhere. Zuri and T'yree looked at T'iang for guidance. He simply gestured for them to follow Martina. They did and he accompanied them. The door closed behind them. Huddled together in a cramped space, Martina activated another control panel and a door opened in front of them to reveal what appeared to be an elevator. Zuri was filled with so many questions, but she kept them to herself. She stole a glance at T'yree who seemed fascinated by what he saw. They filed onto the elevator and immediately wished they had not. It dropped so suddenly and swiftly that she and her husband were left wondering if their internal organs were still inside their bodies.

They instinctively grabbed each other and clung together for the duration of the ride. They never noticed the amused looks from T'iang or Martina.

The elevator plunged deep into the mountain then felt like it changed direction and continued down at an angle. It slowed before coming to a stop. There were a few moments when nothing happened allowing everyone to regain their orientation before the door opened.

Zuri and T'yree let go of each other when they were certain the elevator stopped.

T'iang, unable to contain himself, teased, "You never forget your first."

The comment made Zuri's mood more surly.

The door slid open, and Tameen and Talia greeted them with the Uderran salute. They were accompanied by an individual who smiled broadly at them. He was much older and looked Selemite and Uderran. They were flanked by four guards, each holding what Zuri was sure were weapons. The man introduced himself.

“Greetings. I am Kazi. Welcome to Second Chance Mountain. I hope your transport was not too stressful.”

Zuri’s mood was fed by a sarcastic thought, *Yeah, right. Sure you do.*

“Please, follow us. We have much to discuss.”

“Can we wait until my insides catch up?” Zuri asked through gritted teeth.

“Certainly,” Kazi said.

His ingratiatingly cordial reply further soured her frame of mind.

He waited a few sectons then motioned to the guards for them to stand down but remain alert.

Martina rolled off the elevator, followed by T’iang, Zuri, and T’yree. They were stunned at the sheer scope of what they saw. People. Lots of people going about their daily lives in a cavernous space hollowed out of the mountain.

Everything looked so modern and sleek. Until this moment, Zuri thought what the Uderran engineers had built was state-of-the-art, but these vehicles and buildings made their efforts feel inadequate.

They piled into a waiting vehicle that floated off the ground and had an engine that was as quiet as a whisper. They were whisked away to wherever they were headed next.

Chapter 34

When the hover arrived at the planetarium, everyone got out and headed toward the building. The guards remained outside while the rest of the entourage were ushered inside by Kazi where they were reunited with Der'von and Lolaan. Sitting among them were Siren and Andorra.

Upon seeing a Thouron in the room, Zuri cursed and yelled, "Murderer!" She pushed past T'yree and went straight for Andorra. Siren rose to meet the challenge, but did not need to do anything when Martina stood up from her chair, placed herself between Zuri and the two women, and forcefully uttered three words.

"That's far enough!"

Zuri stopped and stared at Martina. It was difficult to tell if it was the older woman's verbal command or the sight of her standing and walking that kept Zuri from reaching Andorra.

After he recovered from his own shock, T'yree rushed forward and restrained his stunned wife. Zuri was too surprised to resist.

Siren sat back down but was prepared to stand again in defense of Andorra if the situation warranted it.

A squad of guards swarmed the room when they heard the commotion and surrounded the group. Their weapons, set for heavy stun, were all pointed at Zuri and T'yree. Being on the business end of any weapon was not a pleasing experience for him. Zuri seemed ready to defy the odds.

The anger in Martina's voice and the disappointment etched in her face were unmistakable. She surmised her great-granddaughter would be understandably peeved with her, but she seriously underestimated the ferocious hatred she harbored toward Thourons.

"You will comport yourself or you may experience the unpleasantness of waking up in the infirmary."

Sensing her great-grandmother meant what she said, and after she saw that no one else made a move to assist her, Zuri raised her hands in surrender and stepped back from Andorra. She crossed her arms in the Uderran manner of respect and reluctantly bowed. She deliberately faced away from Andorra. T'yree mimicked his wife.

"Apologies," she said.

With the situation seemingly under control, and at Kazi's direction, all but two guards returned to their posts. The remaining two posted themselves on either side of the room. Everyone else breathed a sigh of relief.

Martina sensed her great-granddaughter's emotional wall was down and felt the pure hatred radiating from her. She chose to calm Zuri by a calculated decision to be gruff and redirect some of that animosity toward her.

"Sit down and shut up."

The tactic worked. Martina sensed Zuri's emotional defenses snap back into place as she glared at her.

Satisfied her great-granddaughter was back in control of her passions, Martina continued speaking, giving her full attention to Zuri.

"Everything will be explained and made clearer in due time. When all is said and done, and you still feel the way you do, you'll have your time to speak your mind—and fight whoever you want, if that's your preference. But until then, behave yourself."

There was a long uneasy silence until she was sure Zuri was in full control of her emotions. Then Martina nodded at Kazi to begin the visual presentation.

What was basically a refresher for everyone else was an introduction to T'yree and Zuri. They sat transfixed at what displayed along the walls and ceiling of the room. Because of the severe importance of the information, no one exited the domed amphitheater. It was imperative they were all on the same page. When the presentation reached the current era, Zuri would occasionally glance toward Andorra. After the presentation ended, Kazi stood and got everyone's attention.

Before we continue these proceedings, I recommend we all take a couple of hours to decompress." He paused then said, "For our Uderran friends, that's a couple of mos."

Siren and Andorra used the opportunity to slip out. Zuri watched them go with a strong, curious desire to follow, but she had been cornered by Martina, T'iang, and the rest of the Uderran delegation. She was furious with her great-grandmother.

"Why did you hide from me the real reason why my parents died, and when did you start walking? Or have you always been able to walk?"

"Regarding your parents, they made me promise not to. You know that. They wanted to tell you themselves. As for my ability to walk, that's recent. Thanks to Kazi and his people."

"I should be angry with you. Actually, I am angry with you. Very angry."

"Understandable. I did not expect you to be otherwise."

"And what about you, son?" T'iang asked. "Are you angry with me?"

T'yree hesitated for a moment before he answered.

"Yes. Yes, I am." Always the mediator, he said, "But I am relieved that you are well, father."

He looked at his wife to see what she would do or say next, but Zuri remained quiet. He knew it was taking all of her strength to maintain a semblance of self control. At least she was not physically challenging someone to a fight as she nearly did with the Thouron.

"As you can see," Der'von began, "we are all here because we each possess attributes that will be crucial for the survival of Uderra, the Mountain People, and the Dark Wooders."

"Apparently, that includes the Thourons, I see," Zuri said.

"Yes, it does," Lolaan said.

"And when we resume after the break, we will all find out why," Kazi said. "Whatever preconceived notions we have, I suggest we discard them. Now, I suggest we take full advantage of the time we have remaining before we reconvene."

Chapter 35

The darkness of the night engulfed the area like a black shroud. Since Progensha had no moon, the stars in the Great Beyond were the only forms of illumination available to Nadir. He dared not use his hand-held trenchlight to see his way around. The light from it would have been seen for mectars. He wished he could have used his night vision magnifiers. Unfortunately, the dim light they emitted might be seen by someone close by and reveal his location. So he continued toward his objective using instinct, rote memory, and the positions of the points of light in the sky.

The formless void was both familiar and not. He slowly trekked along as quietly as possible across an open expanse of nothingness. The gravel that crunched beneath his feet was once grass. The whole area was once home to livestock, people, and habitable structures. Now, there was nothing. Mounds of rubble were the only reminders of what once was. An eerie sensation lurked in the pit of his soul as he remembered everything that no longer existed. It was as if he could hear the spirits of the dead accusing him, judging him, condemning him. But something also beckoned him.

Sols earlier, high up in the hills, Nadir had seen something that piqued his curiosity. At least he believed he had. It made him feel unbalanced, unsure, uneasy. He was determined to discover what and why. He cautiously made his way toward a single point in all of the emptiness.

Expertly avoiding contact with caravans and streams of people fleeing Uderra, he crept toward his destination taking a circuitous route. Once he reached the ragged border separating the living from the dead, he traveled only at night and hid beneath camouflage netting of his own design created to blend in with the landscape when the suns cast their light upon the land. Nadir took these times to recalculate his journey and map his movements using a pocket compass to track the suns as they arced across the sky. When the stars appeared, he moved carefully but swiftly toward his objective. A thin layer of clouds hung in the sky. When the suns were at their peak, rainwater poured over the land. They dispersed at night. It was a phenomenon he found fascinating.

Nadir surmised the atmospheric oddity had something to do with the heat from the suns causing the moisture in the air to gather until its weight grew too heavy to remain aloft. The water vapor fell back to the ground as light rain. As the heat from the suns weakened, the coolness of the night air took over and caused the clouds to dissipate. He relied on this repeating weather cycle to make his way across the terrain.

Before the start of each sol, Nadir used the damp soil to dig a hole deep enough for him to comfortably sleep in. He preferred sleeping in the fetal position as the hole could be shallow and small enough to reduce the dirt piles and any giveaway profiles. He lined the bottom with a thin, impermeable membrane, then spread the netting over the depression and remained within it until night. It was solid enough to prevent him from getting soaked by the rain, but porous enough to filter the light and allow air to flow. Anyone surveying the area with magnifiers would have seen nothing but desolate terrain. Under the cover of darkness, he filled the dirt back in and moved on. He repeated this ritual for sols.

During an unusually cloudy night when he was mere mectars from his goal, he thought he sensed movement within close proximity to his location and strained to see in the pitch blackness around him. Unfortunately, the cloud cover blotted out the stars and obscured any shapes he might have been able to make out along the landscape. The only discernable sounds were the misty rain droplets that pattered into the ground as they fell, and the wind as it whispered in the air around him. But he could not shake the feeling that he was not alone.

Nadir gingerly removed his backpack and placed it on the ground, took out his knife, then stretched prone on the ground as flat as he could make himself. His chin rested in a veneer of mud. He wanted to pull out his nightvision goggles, but the lowlight mechanism inside them made their use under current conditions impractical and dangerous. He took short breaths and waited until he could no longer sense danger, then transitioned to a crouch and swiveled his head to try to see and hear anything.

Nadir assured himself it was just nerves and that his mind was playing tricks. He sheathed the knife and reached for his backpack when a slight sting stabbed the side of his neck. He instinctively grabbed the spot and felt a small, embedded object. Suddenly woozy and weak, he dropped to his knees then fell face down unconscious into the mud. A shadowy figure knelt beside his limp body and rolled him onto his back. A second individual nudged him with their foot. When he did not move, the one who reached him first grabbed his backpack then helped to lift the unconscious Thouron and carried him to a waiting transport. Mud was wiped from Nadir's face and scraped off his uniform before he was strapped to a gurney in the vehicle's flatbed. Both people sat in the back beside their prisoner while a third person sat behind the wheel.

The nearly imperceptible hum of the engine was masked by the low whistles of the wind scraping across the rubble on the ground as the hover silently sped off into the night.

Chapter 36

The intermission lasted far longer than Kazi said it would, which was fortunate because it gave everyone time to recover from the tension of the earlier session. Zuri had actually used the respite to discuss matters with Martina. To T'yree's surprise, after a rocky start, the two women amicably resolved most of their differences. Where the two of them were concerned, there were always issues that needed to be negotiated. Sometimes through his mediation but most times without. The only remaining sticking point was Zuri's difficulty processing her feelings about Andorra.

Zuri's position was that Martina should be allowed to harbor ill feelings toward the Thouron considering her people murdered three close members of her family. Or like T'iang said, five, if you take her parents into consideration. Martina's take was that despite what happened, and despite the fact that Andorra was a Thouron, she did not kill her family. The hate she carried in her heart was difficult for her to reconcile, but she fought hard to control it and not let it control her.

Martina was adamant in her support for Andorra. She said that the Thouron made a conscious choice to reject her upbringing and cast off her cultural indoctrination. By doing so, she chose to put herself in harm's way for a noble cause.

Der'von and Lolaan told Zuri she was not alone regarding her feelings about the Thouron, but that they were inclined to defer to the wisdom of Martina and T'iang. Tameen and Talia acquiesced to their bosses.

A sign that the extended break was about to be over became evident when the sound of the main doors being opened caught everyone's attention. Kazi, who had spent the break somewhere other than the planetarium, walked through them. He was accompanied by Siren, Andorra, and another Dark Wooder who had even more exotic features.

Kazi introduced the newcomer as Wraith a male version of Siren. Unlike her, he had a tail and his entire body was covered with a smooth layer of black hair. To Zuri, T'yree, Der'von, and Talia, this newcomer resembled Lolaan and Tameen more than Siren.

Wraith's clothing matched his hair. The only bright colors were his pink nose and gold irises. He greeted the assembly in a low tone that bordered along menacing. He chose to sit behind Siren and Andorra.

If she had not seen the archival records and the planetarium display, Zuri would have thought it uncanny how the inhabitants of the Dark Woods and Mountain People were nearly as varied as the Uderrans.

Where the Travelers were a generous mixture of many ethnic groupings, like her great-grandmother, the Uderrans were dominated by traits of the Plains People like her husband, and the Mountain People seemed to be dominated more by those with gray skin like Der'von and Talia, while Siren and Wraith seemed more akin to Lolaan and Tameen.

Martina's appearance, a blend of Der'von's people and Siren's, lended more credence to the story of the sudden arrival of the Travelers. It was no wonder the Thourons felt threatened. Zuri thought they were the most homogeneous and least diverse of everyone on Progensha. But that still did not give them the right or privilege to dominate everyone else. Especially through violence or subterfuge. They could have mingled like everyone else, but they chose isolation. As far as she was concerned they should have stayed isolated.

While Zuri pondered the exquisiteness of diversity, and how it was all related and interconnected, Kazi continued in his role of host, but instead of standing, he remained seated.

"Now that we are all aware of *what* has brought us together, we will now learn the *why*."

The auditorium darkened and video images of Lin and Piper appeared on a projection screen that rose up out of the floor of the center stage. The shaky video images were recorded from a device Lin held in her hand. She and Piper looked haggard. Their faces were streaked with dirt and their clothes were stained with sweat and what looked like blood.

These images were far more disturbing from the ones Zuri had viewed of her parents prior to this. She wondered why they were not included with the batch Martina initially gave her.

The sounds of heavy booms and violent explosions could be heard in the distance as dirt and dust sprinkled down around them with each thunderous impact. Zuri realized they were in Martina's basement bunker. Lin coughed before speaking.

It's been nearly thirty sols since we left Uderra. The city has been evacuated. Only a handful of stragglers and defenders are left, and they're about to pull up stakes and head out. Unfortunately, we're not among them—and won't be.

She brought the recorder closer to her face and stared straight into the lens.

By now, most of you should know why.

The booming sounds grew louder as more dust and debris fell from the bunker's ceiling. Lin and Piper huddled closer.

For those of you new to the party, we need to tell you we're not natural born Progenshans. We are from planets, worlds, in the Great Beyond. Where we come from we call it space. But what most of you don't know is that we're also from what you call another plane of existence. We call it a universe or dimension. And there's one more thing.

There was another boom that shook the bunker. The single light that illuminated the couple winked off, flickered, then popped back on. After a moment's hesitation, Lin resumed speaking with a bit more urgency.

We're also from the future.

The sound of a nearby explosion rocked the bunker and caused small bits of the ceiling to fall. Lin dropped the recorder and the screen went blank. No visuals, no sound. Zuri's heart pounded hard in her chest. She thought she had just witnessed her parent's final moment when the recording came back on. Both Lin and Piper coughed as the dust filled the air. Zuri wondered why they were not using breathers. She figured they were either lost or damaged. Lin cleared her throat then continued talking.

This might be hard for some of you to understand, but for us, in our universe, the Michael Anderson disappeared one cycle ago, and we first visited Progensha just a few cycles ago. But for you it will be three hundred cycles from now. In other words, what's one cycle for us is five hundred for you. And since we visited Progensha three hundred cycles from now, we know some of what will happen three hundred cycles from now.

Zuri felt a pang of sadness and anger as she watched her mother take a labored breath and wheeze. She wanted to jump through the projection screen and pull her parents to safety. Lin swallowed hard, then continued to explain what she meant.

Unfortunately, we don't know all of what will happen, but we want to pass on what we know to prepare you in case ... .

Lin trailed off, unable to finish her sentence. Zuri reached for her husband's hand and squeezed. Tears ran freely down her cheeks. Seeing her parents this way hurt. She remembered them as vibrant, loving people who instilled in her a sense of pride and discipline that she saw them trying to maintain under dire circumstances. Her soul screamed in frustration because there was nothing she could do. What she was looking at had already happened. Maybe if she had known, she could have thought of a solution. Kept them from becoming martyrs. She struggled with her feelings as she watched Piper point the recorder toward himself and finish the sentence.

In case what we're about to do somehow alters the future.

He continued speaking for Lin.

What we know is that the war with the Thourons will still be going on three hundred cycles from now, and the Uderrans will be leading the fight. Together with the Uderrans will be the Mountain People, the Dark Woods People, the Nomads, and an underground resistance. Unfortunately, we don't have much detail other than that. All the Uderrans and the others know is that some major disaster nearly destroyed the world causing them to forget how things were and lose touch with each other.

Another series of booms and explosions rocked the bunker and more dirt and debris fell around them. Piper dropped the recorder. It fell on the ground facing up and continued to record. Everyone watched as Piper wrapped his arms around his wife to protect her from falling rubble.

Zuri squeezed T'yree's hand tighter. It felt like she was about to break every bone in his hand. He endured the pain for his wife's sake. They watched as Piper picked the device back up, cleared his throat again, and resumed talking.

It's our hope that we can help fix whatever happened that fucked things up. That will mean working with each other and with Andorra and her people. If you can change the will of the Thouron People, maybe you can stop three hundred years of bloodshed. You will all need each other.

Lin regained some emotional control and added to what Piper said.

That's why we chose all of you. We believe you have what it takes to save this world from its own shortsightedness. We worked with Martina in handpicking each of you. You each have unique talents we believe you will bring to the table to stop what is coming. She has a working framework for building a better Progensha.

The booms and explosions were replaced by small arms fire and shouting voices. There was panic in Lin's voice and an increasing sense of urgency.

We know this all sounds confusing, but hopefully your descendants will understand.

The shouting voices grew louder as theThouron troops got closer.

Our time is growing short. This will be our last transmission. Martina will have a copy of it and everything you will need. Listen to her counsel, and you should get through this. May the Goddess be with you. We love you, Munchkin.

The display screen went silent and dark as it dropped back into its position tucked away beneath the stage floor. The desperation, hopelessness, and sadness Lin and Piper exuded made everyone in the room feel overwhelmed with a mixture of conflicting emotions. It quickly became abundantly clear to all that Lin and Piper did not know they were the cause of the disaster. They were the ones who set things in motion.

"By the heart of the Goddess," Zuri muttered out loud, "they died thinking they were helping to save the future when they were the ones who created the one they knew."

"That is correct," Martina said, "And it is up to us to make sure the future they knew still happens."

"But how do we know what we do or do not do will make that come to pass?" Lolaan asked.

"Faith of the heart."

"That's asking a lot, Gran," Zuri said.

"Sometimes faith is all you have. And right now, we have that and the knowledge your parents left behind."

Martina was suddenly overcome with grief, became lightheaded and stumbled. Kazi was immediately at her side, and Zuri sprang to her feet. She waved them away and said she was okay.

“Seeing the recording has increased my sorrow and rekindled memories of my losses. Give me a moment. It will pass. I will be fine.”

She felt responsible for Lin and Piper’s deaths and always would. The feeling of losing them was as strong as when she lost her daughter and granddaughter. But now was not the time to dwell on it.

Zuri did not realize until that moment just how deeply her parents’ deaths affected her great-grandmother.

Martina took a few deep breaths then addressed everyone with the strength and certainty they were accustomed to, “We must begin strategizing ASAP.”

Before Martina could get into a groove, Kazi derailed her momentum. “But first, you must touch base with your constituents before they begin to worry. We can return to these matters in the morning.”

Annoyed at being interrupted, Martina choked back a retort when she realized he was right.

“You are correct,” she said.

He grinned and said, “I know.” Then he extended a hand and asked, “Please, join me for dinner?”

“Don’t mind if I do.”

Chapter 37

Nadir felt a throbbing pain in his neck and wondered why it hurt. He reached for the sore spot but found he could not move his arm. Why could he not move his arm? Had it gone to sleep? Had he fallen and broken it? If he had, why did it not hurt? Only his neck did. Was he asleep and dreaming? That had to be it. He needed to wake up before someone found him lying in the open. He thought he must have been so fatigued that he never dug the trench so he could hide. He needed to dig.

He tried to move and open his eyes, but it was a struggle. Sleep paralysis, he decided. That was it. He was on the verge of waking from a deep sleep. After what seemed like an intense battle to become conscious, his mind cleared allowing him to become more aware of his surroundings. He was not lying on a cold, muddy ground or on his sleep mat. He was dry, on his back, and somewhat warm. He could feel his clothing had been removed. Was he naked? Why was he naked? He could not be naked if he felt warm. His mind swirled with questions until one sobering thought prevailed. He was a prisoner.

Nadir came close to breaking out into a cold sweat. There was no doubt that he had been captured. A prisoner somewhere. He needed to calm down and think. Soft, rhythmic beeping and humming permeated his hearing. When he tried to open his eyes, they felt like they were glued shut. It took great effort to slowly open them to narrow slits. His reward was blurred vision. Nothing was in focus. Nadir laid still until he felt he had better control over his body. His mind raced a mectar a micton, and his heart beat even faster. He took in a few deep breaths to relax his mind. Calmer, he made another attempt to open his eyes and this time succeeded.

He was in a small room barely illuminated by a single light. The sources of the sounds were shadowy machines which lined the walls. He tried to sit up but found his legs, arms, and torso were strapped down. At least it was now clear why he could not reach for his neck. He lifted his head up enough to see he was covered in a sheet. At least he was not naked. Then he felt a surge of anxiety.

"Where am I?"

Nadir heard the question in his mind, but when an electronically altered voice answered him, he realized he had actually verbalized it.

"Do not be concerned with that now. No harm will come to you—as long as you cooperate."

Harm? Cooperate? Had he been captured by the enemy? Or worse, his own people? Whoever they were, showing fear would not be a viable option. Nadir struggled to break free of his restraints. It was a futile effort. He spoke in a tone of voice he hoped implied strength and defiance.

"I demand you release me at once."

"You are in no position to make demands."

He found the courage to display some bravado. Probably a useless move, but one that helped tamp down a growing fear and keep his wits before he lost his mind in abject terror. Was this the fear those poor prisoners felt? he wondered.

"My people will be coming for me. Their retribution will be swift and merciless."

The last half of that declaration would sort of be correct if they were his people.

"No doubt. That is a certainty we will face inevitably, but not now. Your people do not know where you are. Or where here is."

He got the confirmation he sought. At least he was not being held by fellow Thourons. Nadir was sure of it. The only reason his own would have him was if they were convinced he was a liability, and he would have never been permitted to live this long.

"What do you want from me?"

"For you to realize what it is you want from yourself."

That definitely was not a reply he was expecting to hear.

"I do not understand what you mean."

"Yes, you do."

The mysterious voice let the last statement hang in the air without so much as a hint of what was meant by it.

How would anyone know what he understood or not? They would have had to have read his mind.

The voice resumed speaking.

“Deep within your subconscious you know precisely what you want. You are deluding yourself otherwise.”

His inquisitor was playing a mind game with him, he decided.

“I have nothing to delude myself about.”

“Honesty is the best solution to soothing a tortured soul. And yours is screaming for help.”

“I am confused. I swear I do not know what you mean or what you want from me.”

“As I said, I want for you to know what it is you want from yourself.”

When Nadir said nothing else but just stared out at nothing in the room, the voice asked another question.

“What is it you desire most before you die?”

Then, in the blink of an eye, the light went out. Nadir was placed in near total darkness. Except for a few blinking lights on the droning machines, he was left with nothing else but the sound of his thoughts. He called out, “Are you there? Are you there?” But only the machines responded with their rhythmic thrumming and beeping.

Am I about to die? Are they going to kill me now? What do I desire most? To live.

He wanted to live. He wanted to be released and allowed to go on his way. That’s what he desired most at the moment. But that was not what he desired most. What he wanted most was to live a normal life. No war. No fighting. No fearing for his life all the time. He was tired of watching others, who only wanted out of life what he wanted, suffer.

He was now fully awake and highly agitated. Obviously, his captors had no immediate plans of releasing him anytime soon. He was stuck with his thoughts and left pondering the question: What did he want most before he died?

Furious more with himself than with the mysterious voice, Nadir was bothered that escape was no longer his paramount concern. It was the unmitigated gall of his captor to compel him to think of something other than escape that fueled his annoyance.

Nadir loathed the person who posed the question to him. The more he tried to think of other things, the more the question repeated itself in his mind. The Goddess was playing a cruel joke, and he was the hind end of it. He decided to play Her game by confronting the question directly. The sooner he had an answer, the sooner he could get out of wherever he was dead or alive.

Nadir thought of his childhood, his education and upbringing. Average for a Thouron he surmised, but he had always felt he was destined for something greater than average. When it came time to serve in the military, he figured he could do something more than grunt work. He opted for Intelligence, but as he became more immersed in it, the more unfulfilled he felt. The more he thought about it, the more he realized unfulfilled was not the best description. Disturbed was a more suitable word to describe how he felt. Appalled was more accurate.

Initially, he drew pride from the information he gathered and passed on to his superiors. He told himself what he did was for the greater good of his people. He felt a sense of accomplishment when an enemy combatant or civilian was captured and interrogated as a result of his work. He became so good at his job, that his superiors began to trust him with participating in the interrogations. But the brutality and the cruelty of what his commanding officers referred to as sessions, started to chip away at his conscience. His morality.

Nadir no longer saw himself as the righteous soldier fighting a noble cause. He began to see himself as an unwilling pawn in an insidious campaign of relentless barbarism in the name of divine privilege. He reached his limit when he was compelled to participate in the torture-death of an innocent civilian simply because they were not Thouron. The experience left an indelible memory seared into his mind.

The sadistic delight of his fellow soldiers unsettled him. He wanted a way out. He needed a way to escape, but how to do that and where to go eluded him. Nadir was stuck in a cultural conundrum. How could he call himself a Thouron but feel so repulsed at being a Thouron?

There were those who tried to buck the system and effect positive change, but the problem with the system was that it was inherently systemic. Anyone who openly tried to challenge it ended up being labelled traitors to the state and their people. They were severely dealt with. Always ending in their imprisonment and eventual death. Public execution. It was seen as a way to discourage dissent.

Nadir had no intention of ending up that way, but until he could figure something out, he was stuck between what he believed were two massively immovable objects.

He pondered his options. They were slim to none, and the slim did not present itself as viable or survivable. If he were ever fortunate enough to leave everything he had ever known, there would be no place for him to go. He was Thouron. Hated by everyone else on the planet. Nadir knew he would be alone. Live alone. Die alone. And be forever on the run. Is that the life he wanted? He knew he wanted out, but what did he want if he got out? What did he really want?

The machines hummed and beeped their indifference to his conundrum. His restraints kept him immobilized while that nagging question persisted in his thoughts.

What do I want?

The question kept repeating itself incessantly in his head. It lingered like an unwanted guest until it drowned all the sounds in the room. It mocked him. He wanted it to go away.

"What I want is forgiveness, redemption, and a chance to make things right."

The words just flowed from his lips like water rushing over a falls. He stunned himself as he said them. Almost at the same time, it felt like a burden had been lifted from his soul.

"Now how do you feel?" the voice of his captor asked.

Momentarily startled, Nadir asked, "When did you return?"

"I never left."

"Why?"

"I posed a question and wanted you to answer it. I simply waited until you had enough time to think about it."

"But—"

"I answered your questions, now answer mine—unless you need more time to think about it. I can wait."

Not wanting to endure anymore silent torture, he said, "I feel like weights have been lifted off me."

"Do you mean what you say?"

He considered his feelings before he answered. For the first time in a long while he felt unburdened by guilt. He replied, "Yes."

"Now that you have come to terms with who you were, and have accepted who you are, it is time to show you what you can become."

Chapter 38

The last words spoken by the voice were familiar.

Think. Remember. Where have I heard them before?

Nadir combed through his recent memories trying to recall where and when he had heard them. The phrasing was different, but the words were virtually similar.

Then like a flash of lightning, he remembered. He had conveniently forgotten because he had been in an agitated emotional mood when they were spoken. Nadir recalled the conversation between himself, Naron, and Andorra.

At the time, Naron had called his loyalty to Thouron into question following an exchange he had with a commanding officer. Intelligence he gathered was being used to hype up support for a retaliatory strike against Uderra and those who survived the destruction of the vale. He had proposed they fully assess the situation before jumping to conclusions. His suggestion was not interpreted in the manner he had intended. It was insinuated his caution was treasonous. And had been called out for it in front of his entire unit.

He never believed the Travelers, the Uderrans, or any of the other inhabitants of the vale were capable of such widespread destruction. But his people were looking for payback and were unwilling to listen to reason.

Naron could be counted among those who had questioned him. Andorra did not accuse him of treason, but she had both confronted and cautioned him to be mindful of what he said or he might disappear as so many others had.

Now he was worried that those who were suspicious of him were about to make him disappear.

It seemed that Andorra was right. He was once a loyal Thouron, but now he despised the very thing that made him what he was. His actions most likely betrayed him, and soon he was about to become a forgotten victim and vanish as so many others had.

In the midst of his thoughts Nadir heard a new sound. At one end of the room was a door that slid open. Three figures stepped through it. The light behind them masked their identities before the door slid closed behind them. The room was once again engulfed in darkness.

Nadir wished they would just kill him and get it over with.

The three figures stood around his bed. One on either side and the third at the foot. Their faces were still shrouded. The one on his right touched his arm, Nadir's pulse quickened, his body stiffened, and his mouth went dry. His mind was flooded with countless ways they would kill him. He expected to feel excruciating pain. Instead, one of the restraints was unfastened. Then the voice spoke to him and he immediately recognized it. This time it was not electronically altered.

"I told you if you were not careful, you would end up disappearing."

"Andorra?"

"Yes."

"What in the Goddess's name is happening? Have I been captured so you can torture and kill me for disloyalty?"

"No. That will only happen if you betray me and my allies."

"Allies?"

"Yes. We are here to recruit you."

"Recruit me?"

"Yes, to our cause."

"Cause?"

"Yes," one of the two others in the room said. "To stop your kind from committing genocide against everyone not like you."

Light suddenly filled the room and he saw Andorra's companions. One was covered in black hair and wore a black uniform of some kind. They looked neither Thouron nor Uderran but more like a Traveler. The other had similar physical attributes but looked more Uderran. They were the most exotic looking Travelers he had ever seen.

"Are you Travelers?" he asked with hesitant uncertainty laced on his voice.

“No,” the more Uderran-looking one said. “Wooders.”

“Wooders? I have never heard of you. Where do you come from?”

“The Dark Woods.”

“Dark Woods? Impossible. Those woods are dark, thick, expansive, impenetrable. No one lives there.”

“We do.”

“But our intelligence reports—”

“Are flawed,” Andorra said. “Like our belief system.”

Nadir looked at his audience stupefied. Then he looked at Andorra and asked, “How is it you know these ... people? And how do you know our information is ... flawed?”

Andorra replied cooly, “Because I supplied the data that misled the Directorate, and I have been assisting with supporting the underground resistance.”

She released the rest of his restraints then stepped back with her hand on her sidearm. Her companions also stepped back, but neither reached for a weapon. All three just stood watching and waiting for Nadir to decide what to do next. He sat up and stared at all of them as he attempted to ingest this new information. It was disconcerting to not have known what he now knew. It was distressing coming to terms with doubts in his belief system. And it was shocking to realize he was not the person he thought he was. He slumped slightly on the bed.

“You are correct in your assessment of me. I was at a crossroads. I do not like who I was. I am ashamed to admit being Thouron.”

“Never be ashamed of what we are. Be ashamed of those who made us into what we have become. Be angry with those who turned us away from the old ways when we lived and traded in friendship with our neighbors. Be disgusted with those who instilled bigotry and hatred into the very fabric of our culture. Be outraged at injustice and intolerance. Be the catalyst for change for a better Progensha for all Progenshans.”

Nadir appeared to seriously consider her words, but seemed apprehensive and unsure.

"Look," she began, "a while back you asked me if you were transparent. I told you you were to me. I saw the disgust take hold as you witnessed more of the brutality of our people. I saw your temperament change as the war dragged on. You dropped your safeguards making yourself vulnerable. But when I saw how deeply the destruction of the valley affected you, and how reckless your behavior became, I decided to take matters into my own hands and save you from yourself."

Drat! If she saw all that, what did others close to me see?

At least it explained his strained relationship with Naron. They had been childhood friends. Now they were no longer speaking to each other.

Andorra looked hard at him and asked, "Are you willing to forsake all that is wrong with our people? Or will I have to end it for you here and now?"

Now he looked directly at her with total shock at her question. He admitted to himself, and to these three, that he wanted to redeem himself in the eyes of the Goddess and others. Nadir heaved a heavy exasperated sigh and said, "Yes and no."

"Good. Then let us begin your training."

Andorra gestured for Nadir to get off the bed and follow Wraith. She and Siren fell into step behind them. When they walked through the door, they stepped out into what appeared to be an enormous underground cavern to Nadir. It was filled with people who reminded him of Travelers. He was fascinated by the diversity and nervous being in such close proximity around so many people different from him. He felt like a minority.

Siren used Nadir's distraction to whisper to Andorra, "Do you believe he can be trusted?"

Andorra whispered back, "Have I ever been wrong?"

Without hesitation Siren said, "There is always a first time."

Chapter 39

The passage of time inside Second Chance Mountain had a different feel for the Uderrans and Travelers. Due to the artificial lighting, the sols seemed to pass more slowly. Kazi said the living conditions were established by their ancestors to emulate living aboard a starship in the Great Beyond. Their circadian rhythms were accustomed to a pattern started two hundred cycles before.

Since their arrival, Zuri, her husband, and the others had become somewhat acclimated to the change. She did feel a bit annoyed that she was stuck inside a mountain while T'iang, Tameen, and Talia had gotten to return to Uderra. Martina had insisted the rest of them stay to begin the process she dubbed Operation Save Progensha's Future. That translated to attending a lot of meetings and planning sessions. But at the moment, she was doing neither.

Zuri sat in front of a leviathan-sized monitor making googly eyes and weird faces at the screen. Pyperlyn happily giggled and laughed at her mother's contortions as she sat and bounced on the queen's lap during the latest of many video calls. Zuri was checking in on her daughter.

"I see she is being well cared for."

"And why would she not? You say that every time you call."

The queen fixed her gaze on Zuri in what appeared to be a sign she took what was said with great umbrage, "She is being attended to by the best nannies in Uderra."

"I do not doubt that. I was just saying that she looks happy. I miss her."

"The feeling is mutual. She is incessantly asking where her momma and pappa are."

She'ara lifted Pyperlyn and held her up in front of the monitor. Zuri took note of how big her daughter was getting. There was no doubt Pyperlyn inherited the Uderran growth spurt genes from her father. Since Lin and Piper had both been Terran, Zuri had grown up more slowly. A growth pattern considered normal among Travelers. Only those native to Progensha or who had Progenshan genes experienced accelerated development.

"Get a good look," She'ara said. "She is happy, well fed, well adjusted, and well cared for. She is neither ill nor injured. Now, if you do not mind, I would like to get back to enjoying the company of my niece."

Zuri did mind, but she would never say that out loud to the queen. She waved a kiss goodbye before the screen went dark.

"Are you satisfied?"

Zuri turned to face T'yree with a look of complete bliss on her face.

"Yes, I am content—for the moment."

He sighed. With Zuri, there was always a caveat. The potential for something to go awry. He suspected it was her parents' influence. After everything they endured, who would blame them for teaching their daughter to anticipate and expect the unexpected. Their lives had been filled with confronting the unknown. It was a series of unforeseen cumulative factors that resulted in their being stranded on Progensha. But they persevered, adapted, and made the best from what the Goddess gave them. Lin and Piper triumphed over adversity until their good fortune expired.

Zuri and Martina were adversely affected by their deaths, but for vastly different reasons. Zuri, because they were her parents. Martina, because she had adopted them. They were as much family to her as he and Pyperlyn were. And now, being given a new purpose and new challenges, both of them had a renewed vigor and zest for life. Despair was replaced with optimism. The future of the planet was no longer clouded in darkness. The knowledge Lin and Piper left behind offered a slim light of hope. Only time would tell which direction the future would go.

Ever the optimist, T'yree asked, "It's been a few sols since Siren and Andorra left. Do you think they are making progress?"

Ever the pragmatist, Zuri replied, "Depends on whether the Thouron can be trusted. The people must never know we are working with the enemy."

"Former enemy."

Zuri huffed then said, "That remains to be seen. If the people ever find out, we will lose whatever credibility we have, and the Thourons will feel obligated to crush all resistance by any means. By then it might be too late for me to say, 'I told you so.'"

"Let us hope and pray it does not come to that."

Zuri sat quietly for a moment before she asked, "I wonder how the others are faring?"

While T'yree and Zuri discussed progress and trust, Der'von, Lolaan, and their aides engaged in video conferences with their staff.

"Since our return, and the knowledge that others exist outside of Uderra, the desire to leave is greater," Tameen said. "Many want to join our brethren. The opportunity to live among those who share a similar cultural identity is a strong impetus for leaving."

After T'iang, Tameen, and Talia got back to Uderra, they immediately began damage control. Using backdoor channels, they worked at quelling the rumors about their demise, and informed a select few of the true details of why they were gone for so long.

T'iang made several public appearances to assure the populace he was doing well. Tameen and Talia met with trusted members of their respective staffs and informed them of what transpired. Discovering they had genetic cousins was the shot of renewed energy they needed and the incentive to keep things under wraps.

During one of several lively meetings with their staff, Der'von and Lolaan were discussing the pros and cons of leaving or staying in Uderra.

"At issue," Talia said, "is the generosity, hospitality, and acceptance the Uderrans extended to us during our time of need. It is appreciated and should never be forgotten, but at the heart of the issue are the sacrifices they made for us. Many Uderrans died defending Traveler City. We owe them our very lives. To abandon them now, feels ... cowardly."

"The honorable thing to do is stay and assist them," Lolaan said.

"I agree with you," Der'von said, "but a lot of people, now that most have fled, are less inclined to stay. And to force them would be counterproductive."

"A good number of those who remain also still feel it is unwise to stay in the city. Like those who escaped the *Michael Anderson*, they are dispersing to ensure someone continues to survive," Talia said.

She exhaled a forlorn sigh and lamented the plight of the original inhabitants of the city.

"But the majority of those committed to staying despite the danger of what happened in the valley repeating itself are the Uderrans."

"It isn't difficult to understand why," Lolaan said. "They were driven out of their ancestral home in the valley, and now the valley is gone. Uderra is all they have left."

There was a long solemn pause in the discussion before Der'von broke the silence with a question.

"What about our constituents?"

"Split," Tameen said. "However, nearly all have said they will stay and help the Uderrans complete construction on the city's fortifications."

"But if we are to complete the city's fortifications, we're going to need more engineers and laborers," Lolaan said.

"That is what Lady Martina and the others are attempting to rectify," Der'von said. "If we can solicit more support from the Mountain People, and the Dark Woods People, we should be able to complete the work needed before the Thourons move against us."

"That's a big if," Lolaan said. "The success of what we're attempting depends on whether the communication and intelligence network can be effectively implemented. It will be the backbone of the resistance."

"The core component will be developing trust among its partners," Talia said.

"I think you mean to say, if the Thourons can be trusted," Tameen said. There was a snarky tone in his comment.

"I agree," Der'von said. "Relying on so-called Thouron expatriates to update us on what the Thourons are doing is a risky gamble."

"But one *we all agreed* to take," Lolaan reminded them.

"Still doesn't make me feel any more comfortable about it," Tameen said in a tone that was almost a mutter.

"I think that is something else I believe we all agree with," Der'von said.

No one objected.

Chapter 40

Kazi and Martina had spent nearly ten sols debating and discussing the wisdom and logistics of what they loosely called the reunification. After wrangling with the details, surly moods, and objections by T'iang and Siren regarding wording and intent, expressed and implied, they sat in his office and ate their evening meal following a rather tense meeting with mountain and Dark Woods representatives. Much of the time was spent trying to finalize an action plan using the information Lin and Piper detailed in their notes. It was Martina's hope that the couple's knowledge of the future would be the engine that would drive the effort to save Progensha from experiencing a protracted war.

Martina fervently believed that the planet's fate was adversely impacted by the deaths of Lin and Piper. If she had not allowed them to persuade her into fleeing to Uderra, they would be the ones deciding Progensha's future right now based on their understanding of its history. It would be less of a guessing game for them.

Kazi, on the other hand, questioned whether their efforts were actually contributing to fulfilling an unavoidable outcome or diverting it from its intended course altogether.

"I am not saying that we should do nothing and let time run its course," he said. "But what if what we're proposing leads to the future they knew rather than changing it? What if our actions precipitate the deaths of people who should not die?"

He jabbed his fork into a thick, but tender cut of caprine braised in a broth of vegetable stew. Caprine were just one of many abundant species of wild animal native to the mountains. The caprine provided the Mountain People with their food, milk, and clothing. Kazi's people also raised their own domestic stock.

"Are you saying you're giving up on the future of our planet?" Martina asked as she eagerly slurped spoonfuls of an aquatic soup. She surprised them both when the unexpected sound of an uncontrolled burp filled the room. "By the Goddess, apologies," she said, clearly embarrassed.

She dabbed at the corners of her mouth with her napkin and looked sheepishly at her dining companion.

"No need to apologize. I will inform the chef her culinary skills are … appreciated." He smiled then waited a beat before asking if he could address Martina's question.

She continued to sip, but did so more daintily, then nodded.

With a detectable lilt of humor in his voice, he continued.

“No, I’m not saying I’m giving up.” His earlier serious tone slowly returned. “I’m saying having foreknowledge of coming events, and acting to bring them to fruition, could alter the outcome.”

“And knowing of coming events but changing their course could avoid another catastrophe.”

“Or lead to one. You said yourself Lin and Piper refused to insert themselves into the geopolitical landscape for fear of influencing the future.”

“But when they did, it was because they felt they had no choice. They could no longer stand by and watch things spiral out of control. They took the initiative and founded Uderra. A city that exists in their time. Had they not, the Plains People might have become scattered wanderers.”

“But what if Uderra was destined to be founded later than it was?”

“Its founding was inevitable. Sooner or later.” Martina was adamant in her belief that the founding of Uderra would have happened because it existed in the future.

“And what of the destruction of the vale? They knew nothing beyond the knowledge that a great war separated everyone. What happened to the valley brought us together, but is now driving us apart. Is this the first deviation from the path to the future?”

“I believe had I been the one to detonate the bomb, the destruction of the vale would have happened anyway. And the exodus would have still occurred. I would not be a part of the aftermath. Regrettably, they dissuaded me from doing what they did.”

“And now they’re dead. And quite possibly the future they knew as well. What if you were meant to die and they survive? What if the first deviation was you not standing your ground? They would have been in a better position to steer Progensha in the right direction because they had first-hand information. Now all we have is second-hand conjecture.”

Talking about what happened to Lin and Piper threw Martina off balance. She stopped eating and stared at her soup just as a tear fell from her cheek into her bowl. She watched as ripples spread out from the impact point. Then a thought occurred to her. Had the tear come from Kazi or from a drop of liquid from anywhere else, the result would have been the same. Regardless of what produced the ripples, there would have been no change in their reaction to the drop.

“It doesn’t matter,” she said.

“What doesn’t?”

“How we get there or who gets us there. As long as we get there. Lin and Piper left us a blueprint. All we need to do is follow it.”

“There are too many variables to consider.”

“There are too many not to.”

Chapter 41

If Nadir was to play his part in shaping the planet's future, he needed to keep up with Andorra, Wraith, and Siren. That meant high intensity training in hand-to-hand combat, knowledge and versatility in the use of every type of weapon made available to him, and the fine art of espionage. Simply hiding out and observing the movements of others was woefully inadequate.

When you were the one constantly under attack and consistently on the defensive, you learned to hone your skills to be sharper than your adversary.

If your enemy had the tactical advantage, you learned to compensate by devising methods that stymied your foe. Military superiority in the field did not equate to automatic victory. It oftentimes led to overconfidence and failure on the battlefield. The destruction of the vale served to drive that point home to Nadir.

His three instructors were well versed in everything overt and covert. Their skills and expertise made his experience pale in comparison. He felt like he was back in basic training. Siren said the daily drills were necessary to broaden his perspectives, give him the proper skillset to survive in the world he was about to enter, and illustrate the dangerous parochialism of his previous mindset.

During one exhausting exercise, Siren lectured him on how his training was holistic.

"Your daily training is necessary to expand your horizons, give you the proper competencies to survive in the world you are about to become embroiled in, and illustrate the dangerous parochialism of your previous mindset," she told him. "You are one of the softest warriors I have ever personally known."

When she initially told him he was soft, he did not quite know how to take her statement. He had always thought of himself as being a tough individual, physically and mentally–that is until he was exposed to what he had come to refer to as his daily torment.

Wraith rarely said much during sparring sessions other than repeating what Nadir felt was his favorite word: "Again." He trained Nadir relentlessly until he either got it right or Wraith got bored or frustrated. The Felid once confided in Siren that he thought Nadir would be more of a detriment to himself than to them.

Much of Nadir's military service revolved around lurking, observing, and slinking around. That part was easy. It was the other stuff that was hard. Andorra kept insisting they were giving him the tools to ensure his first mission with them would not be his last.

The time he spent with the others showed him how deleterious his people were. The animosity he endured hit him like a sucker punch to the face. He wondered how Andorra dealt with the undercurrent of hostility and the feeling of isolation—not just from being among those not like her, but also from her own kind. She walked among everyone as a perceived equal, but there was an aloofness that encapsulated her like a shroud. Her existence had to be a lonely one, but she bore it well.

His thoughts harkened back to a rather intense encounter he had with Andorra. *We are more of a kindred spirit than you realize*, is what she had said. It did not occur to him until now that she saw something in him that he had not seen in himself. There was a kernel of honor and integrity at the core of his being. At the time, all he felt was disillusionment fed by confusion and uncertainty.

In the early sols following his capture, he was initially skeptical of what he learned and distrusted much of it as psychological indoctrination. He started to come around when he learned that the destruction of the valley was due to a futuristic weapon from another realm. He had always sensed that there was another reason for what happened. He felt vindicated when the actual cause of the disaster was revealed to him. Unfortunately, his superiors were only interested in getting revenge and not getting to the truth.

It also fascinated him that there were worlds and living beings from those worlds living in the Great Beyond. It made their conflict seem all the more insignificant.

Whenever their schedules permitted, Andorra took him to a local playground. They would sit, eat, and watch the children at play. She said it was part of his training to observe more than just the world around him. The more he observed, the more he came to understand that differences in appearance, approach, beliefs, or philosophies need not be perceived as a threat to defend against or an excuse to exploit, subjugate, or destroy. The battle to be fought was not against a group of people, but a fight to change the hearts and minds of those whose ingrained notions were too entrenched to change overnight.

Nadir's training gradually introduced him to other operatives who worked in the shadows of a network which included other likeminded Thourons who were part of a burgeoning resistance. They were tired of the unending cycle of violence and were seeking to end it and forge a new path of peace and cooperation.

His introduction to working with the network came in the form of monitoring a series of intercepted communiques and progressed to infiltration techniques. As much of his training was mental as it was physical. Because time was of the essence, his training was crammed into a tight timeframe. He had to return to his people without raising suspicion. The length of his disappearance had to be believable.

It was not unusual for him to go sols on end without making contact. It was an accepted practice to remain in the field out of touch. Nadir, Andorra, and others in their division were expected to conceal themselves until whenever they felt it was safe to return and report their findings.

Andorra decided enough time had passed after sols of grueling tests and exercises. During one of their infrequent visits to the playground, she said, “I believe you are ready to go back into the field. Do you believe you are ready?”

The success of the planned operation depended upon him.

Nadir reviewed his training and searched his feelings before he said, “Yes, I am ready.”

“Good. The Thourons are preparing for some kind of assault on those who have left the safety of Uderra. Their first targets will be those closest to the hills.”

“How do you know that?”

Andorra sounded a bit skeptical when she answered his question.

“Operatives on the inside.”

He felt foolish after he asked the question because he knew that was the case.

“Are you certain you are ready?”

“Yes.”

She eyed him with what looked to him as doubt and suspicion before she continued.

“The role of the resistance is to thwart it or at least mitigate its severity. Their first goal will be to disrupt communications and delay any attack. The second goal is to delay any Uderran military involvement for as long as possible. To achieve both objectives means they need to ascertain as many details as possible. And that is where your service is required. You are the only one among us with high enough clearance to gather the data we need. Any attempt by me to gather information above my station will draw undue attention."

During Nadir's training, Andorra would furtively shuttle between the mountain and Thouron territory. She fed the military false reports she said Nadir gave her. The intent was to keep the brass from questioning his extended stay in the field and reduce suspicion, while giving her the cover she needed to go back and forth unimpeded.

Unfortunately, the intelligence she was able to gather was inadequate, and her cover was tenuous. The few contacts embedded within key Thouron political and military positions were not enough. No one but Nadir could get close enough to Central Command to make a difference. His previous deployments had him working directly out of Command. So Andorra devised a stratagem to get Nadir close to Thouron power circles.

She claimed she had lost contact with Nadir, and after an extensive search, could not locate him or ascertain any evidence of his whereabouts. It gave her the time she needed to complete his training and to stage a believable escape from captivity. Nadir needed to look like he had encountered some kind of misfortune that would convince any doubters that he barely survived.

On the sol before the first step in the execution of their plan was to be implemented, Andorra stopped by Nadir's quarters to gauge his frame of mind. She knocked and waited to be allowed in. To her surprise, he opened the door himself rather than call out for her to let herself in.

He did not look well.

She was immediately concerned for him.

"Are you alright? Do I need to call a healer?"

"No."

He gestured for her to come in then shut the door when she did. He turned to face her. There was a discernible nervousness in his voice.

"How did you feel the first time you went on a mission? I don't mean on an intelligence-gathering mission, but a direct undercover one."

"Scared dratless."

"How did you get through it?"

"I asked the Goddess for strength and to guide me through it."

He looked down at the floor then back up at Andorra.

"I do not have your level of faith."

"It is not a matter of levels, but whether you have faith in yourself and in Her. She does not care how much faith you have as long as you have it."

Nadir stared for a long moment into Andorra's eyes before he admitted his gravest concern.

"I am afraid." He quickly qualified his comment. "I do not mean I am afraid to die, I am—afraid to die. But I am more afraid I will fail in my mission and jeopardize the lives of others." He faltered. "I am afraid I will disappoint … you."

Andorra saw that his fear was genuine and she felt his confusion.

"Do you want to call off the operation? If you feel that strongly about it, I think I can convince Siren to abort."

"No, that is not what I want. We have worked too hard to give up now."

"Then what is it you want?"

He looked longingly at her. And as he did, she saw the need, the desire, and knew instantly what he wanted before he said, "I want you."

She took his hands into hers and gathered the courage to tell him her secret. Something she was certain would change their relationship. She sighed and said, "There is something about me you need to know. You would not find me appealing because I am … severely scarred."

“I do not care about your psychological traumas.” He realized how insensitive what he said must have sounded to her, and tried to explain himself. “Well, I do. I really do, but they are not the reasons why I do.”

“I was not talking about my mental traumas. I was talking about my physical ones. I am not physically attractive because my body is blemished.”

“I do not care about that. I care about you.”

Andorra let go of his hands, stepped back and slipped out of her uniform. She stood before him totally naked.

“Do you like what you see? Do you like me now?”

She studied his face as he looked her up and down. She looked for any sign of disgust. Andorra was convinced that Nadir would find her physically repulsive and blanch at her wounds. His next move surprised her.

He stepped out of his uniform and stood nude before her. At that moment there was nothing to hide. Their vulnerabilities were fully exposed. Nadir had a few scars of his own, but not nearly as many as Andorra had.

“Are you not repulsed by the sight of me?” she asked.

He cautiously reached out and ran his fingers over her welts. She gasped at the tenderness of his touch. Then he stunned her when he reached for her hands, and pulled her close so his body pressed against hers. Nadir kissed her softly on her lips. A strange and wonderfully new sensation enveloped her. Andorra did not flinch or attempt to pull away. She eagerly reciprocated.

He softly and lovingly caressed her body; she tingled with excitement and anticipation. Her pulse quickened and her breath grew more shallow as they slowly slid to the floor. Andorra guided Nadir to where they both wanted to be. Joined as one. For a few blissful mictons they forgot their worries, their responsibilities, their fears.

They rocked and swayed with careless abandon against each other until they achieved a satisfying rhythm of give and take. Their inhibitions were cast aside. The world around them melted away until it no longer mattered.

For the first time in their lives, they each felt accepted for who they were.

The next sol, they reported to the main medical facility where the mountain medical staff prepared Nadir for his mission. They administered a cocktail of drugs to rapidly reduce his weight. In a matter of sols he looked emaciated to the point of death. They then simulated injuries that would pass the most scrupulous observers and stringent medical scanners.

The final measure was to devise a plausible story that would deflect suspicion. When Nadir was ready, he was dropped off along the edge of the destruction zone so he would be found by roving patrols.

The ploy worked. He was found and rushed back to Thouron for healing care and debriefing as soon as he was deemed fit. The rest was up to him. He would either betray Andorra and the resistance or work against his own. He was in too deep. One wrong move and he would be killed by Thourons who would suspect him of being a traitor or by Thourons who worked within the resistance. The choice was up to him. He opted to feign memory loss when pressed by interrogators regarding his whereabouts during his extended absence.

While Nadir grappled with his new reality, Zuri, Lolaan, Der'von, and Martina embraced theirs.

After some serious debates, the group decided not to inform the Uderran people of the existence of the inhabitants of the Dark Woods. The Thourons were not yet aware of their existence, and the prevailing opinion was their existence should continue to go unknown for as long as possible. They reached a consensus that the less people who knew, the more easily they could accomplish their goals. Those who had already evacuated were considered out of the loop and less of a liability.

The decision to move forward incognito was reinforced when Martina discovered a cryptic entry in Lin and Piper's notes. In it they stated that most Progenshans of the future were unaware of sentient life outside of their world, and the resistance still functioned as an underground network. The entry was enough for Martina to pull back on her plans of full transparency.

Needless to say, the decision was a satisfying relief to Siren and Wraith who preferred that Dark Wooders remain an unknown quantity.

The Wooders, a term they used to refer to themselves, were considered too exotic in appearance and might prove a liability. Siren and her people would provide stealth support from afar. Remaining hidden would also disrupt Thouron efforts to reassert their dominance.

Their presence created an insurmountable enigma and an effective deterrent to full-scale invasion. Any Wooders who did come into contact with Thourons were automatically assumed to be displaced survivors of Traveler City.

It was inevitable the Thourons would eventually discover who was obstructing them, but until that happened, the Wooders would continue to provide logistical support to the resistance. Any assault on the woods would be a futile attempt. The density of the trees was a natural barrier that made it impractical to mount any large-scale attempt to invade.

Attempts to defoliate or burn the woods would result in negligible damage. The inhabitants of the Dark Woods anticipated such tactics and created fire breaks and erected other barriers to thwart any incursions. It all looked natural to the landscape. Nothing looked contrived or artificial. The internal configuration of Wooder territory was a mystery and would remain so for cycles.

As an engineer, Zuri was fascinated by the schematics her parents sketched. Upon her return to Uderra, she established a special unit of engineers. Their sole purpose was to build the things according to her parents' specifications. She was in awe of the structures they detailed. She would have never imagined anything along their size and scale. Three in particular amazed her.

One was a building called a hangar. Its purpose was to house enormous craft that could fly in the atmosphere and in the Great Beyond. But since the Uderrans had not yet invented anything that could fly, her parents said before their arrival, the building was used as a staging area for troops and equipment because there were no flying ships of any kind. In fact, Zuri had already begun working on its construction with her mother believing its sole purpose was to serve as a training facility for military purposes. Not once during the laying of the foundation did her mother mention anything about flying machines.

The second was how massive the palace would become. It was part of an extensive underground complex that supported military installations, research and healing facilities, and the royal palace. It resembled an enormous fortress. Most of which was below Progensha's surface. Despite its size, it maintained a low profile on the surface giving the impression the royals did not live apart or above the average citizen. A large portion of it was composed of bunkers that could comfortably support hundreds of people, areas to facilitate food growth, and workspaces to allow the government to continue to function.

The third was the wall around Uderra had an electronic shield surrounding it that was used to deflect and intercept projectiles. Much of the technology was beyond current standards or understanding, but Zuri reveled in the knowledge that she would be on the forefront of discovering, building, and implementing the technology of the future. It was exciting. Knowing that Kazi's people were willing to lend their assistance in teaching the Uderrans how to build floating chariots was enough.

A corps of technicians, medical personnel, engineers, scientists, and teachers from the mountains emigrated to Uderra to begin work on the city's infrastructure. The group of volunteers that chose to make Uderra their home, resembled Uderrans the most and could easily assimilate into Uderran culture.

The official story was they were a lost tribe of Plains People who broke off from their brethren in the valley, merged with some remnant of Travelers and became cave dwellers who lived high up in the mountains. Following the destruction of the vale, they came down from the mountains and offered their assistance to the Uderrans.

As for Lolaan and Der'von, the fact they were personally selected by Lin and Piper was enough for them to take up the mantle of responsibility and help forge the path foretold. When they returned to Uderra, they immediately began working to establish a more concrete line of communication with the Wooders and Mountainers.

Der'von and his staff devised protocols and implemented safeguards to keep the Thourons off balance and guessing.

After the engineers, medics, and scientists who moved to Uderra from the mountains were settled, the rebuilding began in earnest.

To Martina, the rebuilding of Progensha was underway, and the first installment of her debt to Lin and Piper was being paid.

Chapter 42

As the resurrection of a devastated world began to take shape, the new alliance was about to experience its first major test.

Intelligence reports said the Thourons were preparing to deploy an elite unit of commandos to attack a group of civilians who had left Uderra and found a plot of land they decided to cultivate. Despite skirting the edge of the destruction zone, they made the strategic mistake of settling too close to the Thouron border.

Siren and Kazi dispatched a group of resistance fighters disguised as settlers to warn the people that an attack was imminent and to urge them to relocate much farther away. After presenting some incontrovertible evidence and employing a bit of skilled diplomacy, the leaders of the would-be pioneers were persuaded to vacate their new homes posthaste.

Knowing the newly established little village was under surveillance, Siren's people slowly and judiciously replaced its inhabitants with resistance fighters. The villagers were allowed to take only whatever they could personally carry. They did not want the Thouron observers to suspect an exodus was taking place. Those who left were replaced by an equal number of combatants. For the ruse to work, the substitutions had to be swift and stealthy.

The Thourons needed to be misled into believing they had the element of surprise on their side. The resistance fighters worked around the clock moving the villagers out and replacing them with their own soldiers.

Expecting the vanguard of the commandos to be equipped with night-vision magnifiers, the same evacuation tactic used during the sol was used at night to reduce suspicion. So as villagers left and were out of range, an equal number of Siren's volunteers replaced them. It was imperative to give the impression that hunters and foragers were going out looking for food and supplies then returning.

Key components of the subterfuge were Andorra and Nadir. Nearly fully recovered from his manufactured injuries, Nadir, along with Andorra, was assigned to accompany the Thouron troops deployed to raid the village.

The greatest obstacle to their plan succeeding was Naron. Central Command selected him as the senior officer in charge of the operation. It was believed since the three of them had a proven record of achieving mission goals and getting results, they would be the ones to lead the first military mission since the destruction of the vale.

Their orders were to decimate the settlement and take hostages to interrogate. Central Command was looking for information that would allow them to exploit any weaknesses in Uderran defenses.

Andorra knew "interrogation" was the Thouron code word for torture. She was determined not to let that happen on her watch—especially to civilians. It was often said the first casualty of war was the truth. But in Andorra's mind, the first casualties of war were the people least able to defend themselves. Civilians. And often the most sadistic individuals were assigned the task.

Though Naron did not necessarily fit that category, he nonetheless had a ruthless nature and certainly no love for anyone not a Thouron or suspected of being an enemy of the empire. His suspicions about Nadir never faded. The long absence exacerbated the doubts he had of his former friend. Andorra felt it was going to be difficult trying to prevent the slaughter of innocents while not revealing themselves as resistance fighters embedded within a highly trained band of assassins led by an untrusting commander.

As the first light from the Progenshan suns peaked over the distant skyline, the Thouron commandos were set to descend upon the village below their observation post and wreak havoc upon the sleeping villagers. Andorra crouched at her post awaiting Naron's orders. Her concerns of whether the operation would succeed or fail were compounded by the uncertainty that Nadir would turn on her. If that happened, Naron would be alerted to her ruse and discover her true intentions before the operation could be carried out. The situation could spiral quickly out of control as a result with her being killed on the spot, or dragged to the capitol for public humiliation and then executed.

She had mentally prepared herself for either possibility. Her good fortune was bound to run out sooner or later. She prayed that when it did, she had done enough to earn spiritual redemption to placate the Goddess. Her thoughts were interrupted by Naron's voice. He spoke in a low tone, concerned that anything louder might carry in the stillness of the subdued light.

"Okay, people," he said. "Line up."

The full unit stood in line at attention while Naron paced back and forth. Their eyes were locked straight ahead, not on him. The stars in the sky overhead were slowly being replaced by the glow of the first sun as it crept over the horizon. There would be no need to use their night vision magnifiers when it was time to move on the villagers. The attack would be swift enough to overtake the villagers as they slept. Bulky headgear would inhibit movement and slow the unit down.

Naron paced up and down the line as he addressed his troops.

“The time has come to get revenge on the enemy.”

He laid out their attack plan.

“We will divide up into squads and surround the pathetic mongrels. All we need are two captives. Do you get my meaning?”

In unison, they all said in hushed voices, “Yes, Commander.”

“Good.” He was insufferably pleased with himself. “Nadir.”

“Yes, Commander?”

“You are with me. The rest of you, follow your squad leaders. Move out.”

Andorra noted Naron was having way too much fun in his role. She also surmised he wanted Nadir nearby to keep an eye on him in case he exhibited any treasonous behavior. Nadir felt the man he once called friend was too deeply immersed in his role.

As they descended the steep hills and raced toward the village, Nadir was suddenly filled with mixed emotions.

He wondered if he had made the right choice. He asked himself if he could be the person he wanted to become or revert to the person he had been. Unfortunately, he did not have the time for an internal intellectual debate. When Naron gave the attack order, all manner of underworld ugliness surfaced.

Believing they had the element of surprise, Naron’s team found the situation had turned instantly nightmarish for them as the villagers fired first.

The Thourons were immediately thrown into disarray.

“Take cover!” Naron ordered.

Taking cover meant seeking protection behind a few trees and a handful of boulders. Not much to protect Naron's unit from the onslaught. Before his troops could push deeper into the more heavily forested section, they were confronted at the edge. It was more of a no man's land with few places to hide. There was a sizable gap of open area between where the outcropping ended and the tree line began.

What the drat went wrong? Naron wondered. The operation should have gone perfectly. He reasoned there were other factors at play here that had not been considered—or the intel was faulty. These people were not shagnots ripe for the slaughter, but fully armed and highly efficient warriors.

Naron and Nadir dropped to the ground to reduce their chances of being shot and searched for anything that could provide adequate protection. They managed to find a large boulder next to a small tree to take cover behind.

What started as a coordinated assault quickly dissolved into a quagmire. The battle raged for at least a mos as each side fought to get the upper hand. Sporadic gunfire rang out in the decreasing darkness. The morning sky brightened enough for the soldiers of each side to visually see each other clearly. A fortunate few found cover. Others were hopelessly left unprotected in a clearing and were gunned down. Amid the rat-a-tat of gunfire, were the moans and screams of the wounded and the dying.

Andorra fired her weapon at the unsuspecting Thourons, ducked and rolled for cover then popped up and fired again before she crawled to a new spot. She moved swiftly so those who became aware of her tactics could not get a good shot off to take her out. They inevitably became targets of the resistance fighters.

Andorra crawled along the ground making herself a harder target to lock onto. She would take down a few commandos then dive behind a tree or boulder. The pop, zing, and ping of weapons fire, and the sound of ricocheting bullets slowly subsided, but not before her luck ran out.

She was using the trunk of a fallen tree as cover when a bullet tore through her right forearm causing her to drop her weapon. A second slug passed through her shoulder knocking her away from the tree. A third ripped through her right leg. She fell hard on the ground in unbearable pain. Andorra barely heard the footsteps approaching before she heard the angry voice.

"Traitor!"

She looked up, choking back sobs between rapid breaths, and saw Naron standing over her. His face was full of anger. His eyes were filled with fury. His sidearm was pointed at her while he quaked with rage.

Naron was on the edge of losing control before he asked, "Do you know what you have done?"

Barely able to speak because of the pain from her wounds, Andorra defiantly nodded and forced herself to say, "Saved innocent men … women, and … children from … needless slaughter."

Naron's full attention was focused on Andorra. He was no longer concerned about the bullets whizzing past him. He was totally oblivious to the world around him. Nothing mattered more than making her pay for her treachery.

Naron let loose an unholy guttural growl of utter contempt then raised his pistol toward her head. She closed her eyes expecting to die just as the loud explosion of a gun being fired filled her head. Accustomed to feeling every type of pain imaginable, she was surprised she felt none. Andorra wondered if she was supposed to. Maybe her death was instantaneous and she was now with the Goddess or in the Underworld. Then she heard the sound of something like a body hitting the ground. She opened her eyes to discover she was still alive.

Lying on the ground next to her was the lifeless body of Naron. The visceral look of hate and anger she remembered seeing on his face before she shut her eyes was replaced by a permanent expression of shock and surprise. A moment later she heard a grunt and then a sigh before she saw Nadir drop his gun, grab his gut, and then slump to the forest floor before falling forward onto the blood-stained ground.

Andorra found the strength to drag herself over to him and checked for a pulse. It was weak but detectable. She gasped a painful breath of air, let it out, then collapsed onto his unconscious form.

Chapter 43

The rhythmic sounds of hums, beeps, and electronic pulses were indicators to Nadir that he was still among the living. Whether he was in the custody of the resistance or his people remained to be seen. But since it was obvious that he was still breathing, his best guess was he was in the hands of the resistance.

He was lying on his back; his hands were not bound so he carefully reached for his stomach and found thick bandages wrapped around his abdomen. His gut felt like it was on fire. Taking a normal breath was tolerable. Taking a deep breath was next to impossible. Goddess forbid if he had to cough or sneeze. Any life-saving surgery would be immediately undone.

At least I'm not a Thouron prisoner.

Nadir opened his eyes and saw he was in a brightly lit white room. He surmised it was one of the healing centers within the mountain. He tried to sit up, but got dizzy making the effort, and winced as a dull ache shot through him. Drugs, no doubt, were tamping down the worst of the pain. So he just laid back and tried to recall the battle and what led up to it.

He remembered having second thoughts about being there and about what he wanted to do. Why was he about to protect people who hated his guts? Because his people gave them no other choice, he reasoned.

Why did it matter to him so much? Because he believed there was a better way. Then there was the question of how was he supposed to protect the villagers without revealing that he was working against his own people? And could he do it without getting killed in the process? The details were a bit fuzzy. All Andorra said was to figure something out.

When Naron ordered the unit to attack, Nadir's doubts became moot. His solution was finding a place to take cover and fire his weapon into open space. But with Naron clung to him like another part of his body, faking it was difficult to do. The thought of firing upon his own was not as difficult as he thought it would be, but shooting them in the back as they charged forward or hid behind trees and boulders was a line he was not willing to cross. He still needed to live with himself. Apparently, Andorra was quite comfortable with who she was. And that person is who Naron took issue with.

When he saw her shoot her own, he became enraged and fixated on her. Seemingly ignoring that they were in the middle of a firefight, Naron planted himself on one knee, steadied his aim at Andorra and fired. He was highly rated with a firearm so the three shots he took were placed where he wanted. He was making her suffer before he released the round that would end her life.

As she fell to the ground, he calmly got up and walked toward her. Naron stood over Andorra with his weapon pointed at her. He was either totally oblivious to the projectiles whizzing and zinging past them or he no longer cared. When a slug blasted the bark off the tree next to his head, he did not so much as flinch. He was focused on Andorra.

Near hysterics, he berated her and said she was a traitor. Naron had lost all sense of his surroundings when he asked her if she had known what she did. After she acknowledged that she had, he totally lost his grip on reality. When he pointed the gun at Andorra's head, Nadir knew then that he had to do something. So before his former friend pulled the trigger, he pulled his.

Immediately after discharging his weapon, he felt a sharp pain in his abdomen. He recalled dropping his firearm and grabbing at his midsection. He barely remembered falling to his knees or collapsing to the ground. He had no memory of anything after that until he woke up in the room.

His thoughts next turned to Andorra. *Is she still alive*? He needed to find out. But how was he going to do that when he did not know where he was or whether anyone would know who Andorra is? He called out.

"Is anybody here?"

Saying just three words hurt almost as bad as the bullet that landed him here. He was winded. He made a second attempt then gave up. He laid in silence waiting for someone to come by and answer his questions. No one did. Moments later, he was overcome with fatigue and drifted off to sleep.

When Nadir woke again, he sensed he was not alone. He fought to open heavy eyelids. When his vision cleared, he saw individuals in white healing garb moving about.

His throat felt restricted and dry; he summoned what little strength he could and asked in a weak, scratchy voice, "Where is Andorra?" He barely heard himself speak. He was not sure if he actually spoke the words or merely thought he had.

None of the healing staff answered, but a feminine voice nearby did.

“She will live.”

He turned his head to face the direction of the voice and looked directly at Siren. She wore her obligatory brown robe and customary unreadable expression. Her vocal cadence reflected her normal unflappable demeanor.

Siren observed the obvious look of instant relief wash across Nadir’s face when she told him Andorra was alive.

“You are fortunate you chose sides wisely. We dispatched everyone but you and Andorra.”

“Fortunate?” He grimaced.

“Yes. You were shot by our best marksmen. No vital organs were damaged.”

He took a shallow breath.

“How … how would you know?”

Nadir painfully exhaled.

“Because it was I who shot you.”

A look of surprise etched itself onto his face. Followed by a veneer of anger that was replaced by one of puzzlement. His expressions were underscored by a question.

“Why?”

“To maintain the illusion and protect your cover.”

“You could not have chosen a less painful way?”

“No.”

“What if I had betrayed you?”

“We would not be speaking to each other now.”

"Oh."

"What if I had not pulled the trigger?"

"You and Andorra would still be alive and your commander would still be dead."

After digesting what Siren said, Nadir asked about Andorra again.

"She is resting comfortably and is out of danger. The healers were compelled to induce an artificial sleep to aid in her recovery. She was revived earlier this sol."

Siren watched another wave of relief ripple across his face before she said, "Just as you were."

Now he reflected a look of confusion.

"If no major organs were damaged, why was I in an artificial sleep?"

"The projectile severed an artery. It needed to be repaired before your wound could be healed."

"Impossible. That kind of surgery is beyond the abilities of Thouron healers."

"Not beyond those of the Mountain People."

Nadir paused and pondered what Siren said. Surely, his people could learn from hers if they were not so narrow minded.

"How long have I … we been here?"

"Ten sols. Now I suggest you do what the healers recommend to curtail your convalescence."

As a mild expression of satisfaction sculpted its way onto his face, Siren made a mental note to teach him the delicate art of facial camouflage before she left him alone with a cadre of healing personnel attending to his recovery.

He woke early the next sol to the sound of knocking on his room door. Forcing himself fully awake, he said, “Enter.” The sound of his voice seemed distant and weak to his ears.

The bright light from the hallway outside his room obscured the silhouetted figure who limped in and stood at his bedside. She leaned on a crutch.

“The healers tell me you are recuperating nicely,” Andorra said.

In a stronger voice closer to normal he said, “As are you.”

Andorra adjusted her stance to something a bit more comfortable before she said, “I want to thank you for saving my life.”

“You are welcome.”

“Now I owe you.”

He smiled and said, “I think we can work something out.”

A brief awkward pause hung in the air between them before Nadir filled the silence.

“Tell me something.”

“What?”

“How was it that you had no problem firing on your own people?”

A twinge of irritation seeped into Andorra’s voice.

“Those commandos were not my people. My people do not maim, murder, or torture. My people do not harm civilians—or prisoners.”

She paused and took a breath. Her eyes narrowed to angry slits.

“It may seem callous to you, but they had every intention of massacring the villagers. I will no longer sit by and turn a blind eye to wholesale slaughter or minor injustices. Naron and his troops got what they deserved.”

Andorra paused her verbal onslaught long enough to catch her breath. She shifted her stance, cocked her head slightly to one side and then asked, “Are you having second thoughts about joining the resistance?”

“No.”

“Are you having second thoughts about me?”

“No.”

She sighed.

“Maybe you should,” she said.

“Why?”

“Because I am damaged goods.”

“If this is about your scars–”

“No, it is about a guilt burden I carry.”

She drew in a deep breath then let it out as she explained why.

“Many cycles ago, when I was still in infantry, I was on a mission. We were told an enemy unit was about to stage an attack on our position. We were ordered to engage and neutralize. The so-called enemy unit was a group of refugees fleeing the war zone. They were civilians. Mostly women, children, and elders.”

Andorra shuddered as she relived the memory.

“I told myself I was being a good soldier and was just following orders. We were told it was for the good of the state, but I was haunted by the carnage. The waste of precious life. Those people were no threat to us. They begged us to spare them, but we did not. A few of my so-called comrades derived sadistic pleasure from the slaughter.”

She paused as the memory of the event worked its way through her mind. It was hauntingly vivid; burned into her conscience as if it had happened only sols ago.

“I requested a transfer to intelligence hoping I could do some good there.”

Tears freely streamed down her cheeks as she spoke and sniffed loudly.

“I promised myself then that I would never be a part of something so vile ever again. So, no, I did not have a problem shooting those murderers."

Andorra struggled to regain her composure before she asked Nadir a pointed question.

“How did you feel when you pulled the trigger?”

Without hesitation he said, “Justified.”

“And now?”

“Content.”

Chapter 44

"This is absolutely fascinating," Zuri said.

She was sitting at her workstation in the front room sipping a hot cup of jamocha and glued to the data on its screens.

"What is?" T'yree asked. He was in their bedroom busy getting Pyperlyn dressed.

"These structures from the schematics and blueprints my parents left behind. They're remarkable."

Zuri's attention was diverted by a giggling, naked toddler who sprinted out of the room with her father in hot pursuit. She noted her daughter was actually quite fast and agile for someone still learning to control her balance.

"You know," Zuri said, "if you give her a treat while you *attempt* to dress her, she might be more cooperative."

The frustration clearly evident in his voice, T'yree said, "You mean a bribe?"

"Yes, if that's what you want to call it."

"I tried that. She took it and dashed off. She is getting more like you with every sol."

Zuri plucked up her daughter before she got too far out of reach, kissed her forehead, then handed the former fugitive to her father. There was no doubt in anybody's mind that Pyperlyn had inherited the Uderran growth spurt gene. Zuri could definitely feel the added strain on her muscles.

"Well, you knew what I was like when you asked for my hand. You should have figured on our offspring inheriting those traits. You knew my parents, and you know my great-grandmother. What were you thinking?"

"I was so smitten with you, I did not think. I was infatuated with all of your wondrous beauty, smarts, and charm."

Zuri blushed. She never understood what he ever saw in her. Unlike other females he could have sought after, she was not the refined aristocrat he could have settled down with. She was rough around the edges and nowhere close to sophisticated. But, apparently, she had a quality that hooked him.

“Careful there, big guy, or you just might end up with another one of her.”

She pointed directly at Pyperlyn.

T’yree smiled and said, “That is a chance I would be willing to take.”

With his daughter, now bundled in a towel, securely wrapped in his arms, and munching on her treat, he walked over to look at the building schematics on the screen of Zuri’s workstation. She had three large video screens attached to the unit.

Though he did not have nearly as much experience as Zuri in understanding what he looked at, she had taught him how to read construction plans, so he was not totally clueless about what he saw. He was also impressed with the sophistication and the elegance of the designs.

“Amazing.”

“I know, right? Everyone in the engineering corps is thrilled about it. Current construction projects have been modified to incorporate these drafts. This stuff is beyond anything we could have ever imagined.”

“What of the perimeter wall?”

The excitement in Zuri’s voice grew even more palpable. She barely contained it.

“Nearly complete. If it wasn’t for the mountain engineers, we wouldn’t even be halfway finished. They have developed techniques we haven’t thought of. The next phase will be to install something called a force field, or force shield, or force something. They’re even showing us how to harness the planet’s thermal energy, and to recycle to reduce waste.”

The last time he had seen his wife this happy was before her parents died. He was happy for her. At least she was now focused on something that renewed her passion for life.

“Enjoy,” he said.

“I am.”

“Let me get this little menace dressed before she outgrows her current set of outfits.”

His comment got a chuckle out of Zuri.

“You do that.”

T’yree kissed his wife and left the room to get Pyperlyn dressed. Zuri went back to studying the schematics.

She was particularly interested in the structure called a hangar. Despite what her parents told her, she found it difficult to imagine craft that could fly in the air, let alone in the Great Beyond. But the thing that perplexed her the most was how immense the ship had to be for something even larger to accommodate it.

She was cross referencing some of her parents’ personal logs with the construction information when she noticed a file size discrepancy. The total number of data bits did not match the number of files in the detailed list. After doing some digging, Zuri discovered a hidden file contained within Lin and Piper’s notes. It was encrypted.

She tried everything she could think of to crack the code and reveal the contents. Nothing worked. Then she hit upon an idea.

What if the mountain clan could decode it for her. Their science and technology was way more advanced than Uderra’s. She contacted Kazi and requested help.

More than happy to oblige, he agreed to run it through their systems. She sent him the file through a secure transmission.

A couple of mos later, he got back to her. They were able to get past the encryption. Kazi transmitted the data over a secure frequency, and Zuri was delighted to read her parents’ personal notes, their innermost thoughts. Apparently, they never got the chance to delete and destroy these entries. At least that is what she thought until she found a subfolder with her name on it. She was completely stunned when she opened it and a video began to play.

Both her parents appeared together in the video, but it was her mother who spoke.

Hi, Munchkin. If you're viewing this, then we can safely assume you have gotten over your grief, shock, and anger, and have begun to forgive Martina–if not us. We hope that in due time, you will find it in your heart to forgive us. We never wanted it to end the way it did. We wanted to see you shine and come into your own, and watch our grandchild grow up.

Lin paused the playback for a moment to collect her thoughts and calm her emotions. When she regained control, she resumed watching the video.

Remember when we told you where we came from, and to never tell anyone we told you? Well, there is one more thing we want to tell you that no one else should know. We wanted to leave you with a little piece of us that you can carry with you for the rest of your life. There is a hidden pocket in your favorite stuffie. In it you'll find some interesting things about us. We hope you cherish them as much as we cherish you.

It looked like the video was about to end when Piper capped off the message with one final comment meant to soothe her mind.

Oh yeah. One last thing. Even though we're gone from your life, remember, in another time and universe, we're still alive. The span of five hundred cycles on Progensha is equal to one to us in our universe.

We love you, Munchkin. Very much.

They both blew kisses then waved before their images faded to black.

After she sat through a tearful moment of introspection while staring at the blank monitor, Zuri got up and walked to the main bedroom and retrieved a stuffed triquadi from her collection of stuffies. She absentmindedly brushed its back with her hand. Her mind was immediately flooded with childhood memories.

The toy was a lifelike facsimile of a breed of Progenshan dog. Its simulated fur was black, dotted with brown spots. Atop its massively round head were two pointy ears, which were offset by a protruding snout and two penetrating ocean blue eyes. A toned muscular body was supported by four short legs that rested on feet sporting three toes each. A spiraled tail as long as its torso completed its appearance. A person had to look hard to tell the difference between it and the real thing.

Grateful that T'yree had taken their daughter out for a stroll around the property, Zuri examined the toy and located the secret pocket. Inside she found handwritten notes with information about the universe her parents came from, the war they fought, and data regarding the ship they served on. But the most surprising piece was a hardcopy image of her parents. It was encased in some sort of clear waterproof seal. They were posing with their friends in front of what she presumed was their ship. It was enormous. She understood why the hangar was so large.

Zuri ran her hand along the face and edges of the picture attempting to get a tactile sense from the photo and felt a deep pang of loss. Then she clutched the picture and held it against her chest.

Through teary eyes and mild sobs she muttered to herself, "You're out there somewhere right now. Still alive, living in another universe, another time, another place."

Her mind started to work overtime. She began to consider the possibilities and weigh her options. If her parents found a way to traverse time and cross the boundaries between alternate planes, then maybe she could find a way with the help of the mountain engineers, her parents' notes, and help from the Goddess.

Martina would have said the Goddess did not work for her. It was the other way around, but Zuri did not care. She knew she was not on the Goddess's favorites list, but figured she might be able to work something out.

"I will find a way to reach you and warn you of the danger. It may take cycles, but I will find a way—even if it means my never being born."

Chapter 45

The Thouron attack on the village Nadir helped thwart was the first of many. His participation in keeping civilians safe from the ruthlessness of his people strengthened his resolve and gave him a clear path to discovering exactly who he wanted to be. He did not doubt or question his choices.

Nadir's transformation was complete. He became the person he wanted to be. If any misgivings did threaten to creep back into his subconscious, he would simply visit a playground and watch the children play. They had not a care in the world or any expectations other than how much fun they would be allowed to have. It helped to assure him that violence against the innocent and their exploitation were the true enemy. There was no place for ethnic intimidation. Though they all looked different from each other, they were all Progenshan. Children of the Goddess. If She had favorites, it was Her decision to make, not theirs to make for Her. To think or do otherwise was presumptuous and arrogant. He was committed to a cause.

Andorra had come to terms with who she was and who she wanted to be long before Nadir. She firmly believed in justice, fairness, and equality and worked hard to make it a reality for others. So much so that she was committed to dying to ensure others got a fair chance in life. Disagreements and arguments were part of Progenshan nature. What should not be a part of it, as far as she was concerned, was intolerance and the prejudiced attitudes her people had toward others.

Together with Siren, Wraith, Kazi, and Nadir, Andorra committed herself to eradicating bigotry anywhere she could. Their hard work and dedication inspired others to join the resistance. The ultimate goal was to mold it into a formidable entity and viable deterrent against tyranny.

Based deep inside the mountains, the burgeoning movement had the potential to become an effective network for change. Defending displaced groups from across the valley or anywhere on the planet. Maintaining their shadowy existence underscored the eventual decision to remain a mystery organization and work in the gray areas that others could not. It was the primary rationale used to withhold making their presence known to the Uderrans. It was decided the less its citizens knew, the better.

But the resistance continued to maintain a tenuous working relationship with Thouron expatriates. Despite the danger of doing so, the long-term payoff was incentive enough to attempt to make it work.

Because of the cultural, social, and economic ties predating the birth of the Thouron Empire and their supremacist ideology, several communities of individuals existed on the outskirts of the Thouron border that were negligibly affected by military incursions or strong-arm political policy. They were the descendants of those who interacted with the Plains People and the Travelers in the early sols before the Thouron influence took hold. Their allegiances depended on how they were treated. Some, due to their perceived ethnicity, were treated more favorably than others. The ones treated less favorably were disparagingly referred to as "Discards" and "Rejects" because of their mixed heritage.

They were the children and grandchildren of those victimized by predatory sexual violence toward non-Thourons or were the result of volunteer couplings by people who were able to transcend perceived differences and did not give a drat about what the Thourons thought.

These groups were, more often than not, marginalized. To most Thourons, Discards were merely a necessary inconvenience that served a strategic purpose. Reject communities were viewed as nothing more than security buffer zones between the Thourons and everyone else.

Many groups were granted dispensations and allowed restricted access to selected aspects of Thouron culture which enabled them to improve their economic status, be granted assigned social privileges, or serve in the military—always through conscription.

The latter proved to be the most divisive. While there were those who saw their restricted participation in Thouron culture as the first steps toward eventual assimilation, others felt they were being used as nothing more than fodder. They believed they would never be fully accepted, and resented their status and abhorrent mistreatment within the Thouron social structure.

These were the operatives Andorra and Siren sought to recruit if the resistance was going to have any impact in standing up to Thouron injustice. Referred to as "Passers" because their physical characteristics were indistinguishable from an average Thouron, they risked their lives by willingly embedding themselves into Thouron culture in order to dismantle its systemic discriminatory institutions and practices from within.

Their ostracization and discontent were the foundation needed to give birth to the next generation of sleeper cells similar to the ones that once operated along the periphery of Traveler City. The lessons learned from them were applied and modified to adapt to the latest Thouron tactics.

The Thouron Empire, still in its infancy as a nation state, was poised to wage a relentless, protracted war for global dominance. It was destined to morph into diametrically opposed factions as the cycles marched on.

On the other end of the spectrum was the city-state of Uderra. Its growing pains manifested themselves through bickering and infighting that threatened its stability. The disappearance of an entire ecosystem and the resulting backlash threatened to rip apart a promising future, if it were not for the headstrong nature of one woman with a direct connection to the past and the future.

"I don't care how you do it, just make sure it's done," Martina said. "They left on their own volition, in spite of cautions to the contrary. They *do not* get to dictate terms or bully their way back."

She was talking with Der'von and Lolaan about resettlement issues. They sat at the debate table in the Uderran council chambers. With just the three of them in the big space, their voices echoed within the hallowed walls.

In the wake of growing Thouron attacks, some of those who left Uderra demanded to be allowed back. The main bone of contention was with returnees who wanted their old neighborhoods and tracts of land, which they vacated. Much of that land was now occupied by immigrants from Second Chance Mountain. And there was no way they were going to be displaced or deported. Their very presence was key to the city's survival.

It became a daunting challenge to relocate the returnees—especially those who felt they were entitled to the spaces they abandoned during the Exodus.

Martina instructed Der'von and Lolaan to hold their ground and give preference to the new immigrants and remind the rest that they forfeited the right to any land they previously owned when they chose to leave. She suggested dangling some prime real estate outside of Uderra's physical borders closest to the city as incentive. They would not be within the walls of the city, but they would still be ideally situated to be protected by Uderra.

Der'von and Lolaan pitched the idea as a first-come, first served, incentive to appease the most obstinate groups. Nothing worked until Martina got personally involved and reminded the most vocal troublemakers they had argued her down and rejected her urges to stay in the sols following the destruction of the valley.

Some of the negotiations, if they could be called that, came close to diplomatic meltdowns, but Der'von's reputation as an intimidating negotiator and Lolaan's expertise in reaching compromises helped to resolve some pretty nasty disputes. Lolaan's idea to dig up recorded council debates and replay their own recorded words back at them helped.

Martina used those small victories as examples that she, Lin, and Piper had made a wise decision selecting Der'von and Lolaan as worthy successors to carry the mantle of responsibility in leading Uderra and the rest of Progensha into a promising future.

When some normality finally began to take hold in Uderra, Der'von, Talia, and most of those of Selemite heritage made the decision to leave the city. The urge to join their brethren in the mountains was strong. So they took up residence in the Mountains and allied themselves with the Mountain Clan.

Lolaan, Tameen, and those mostly of Felid ancestry made a similar choice. They moved to the Dark Woods, made it their home, and allied themselves with the Dark Woods Clan.

For Lolaan and her constituents, there was one important caveat. Their silence. They had to swear to never reveal the existence of the Wooders. They also swore to never return to Uderra.

Needless to say, Martina was greatly disappointed when the Selemites and Felids departed. The unified Progensha she envisioned did not appear to be taking shape as she hoped. She wondered if she was witnessing the beginning of the schism that divided Progensha.

Martina sat in her room going over some notes and drowning her woes in a cup of thicket tea when her comm unit chirped. She glanced at the screen and saw the ID was from T'iang.

"To what do I owe the pleasure of this call?"

Her mood was not as inviting as her greeting sounded.

"I am just checking on you to see how you are doing."

“For the first time in a long time, I am unsure of myself. I thought all of the pieces were falling into place, but now I am not so certain they are.”

“Sounds like you are second guessing yourself.”

“With the absence of Der’von and Lolaan, I am left wondering if I was too heavy-handed in insisting on following the blueprint Lin and Piper left behind. I fear the Goddess is punishing me for being overzealous.”

“I do not view it as a punishment.”

T’iang paused and looked pensive for a moment. His face reflected a painful memory before he resumed speaking.

“The Goddess sent Lin and Piper to us for a reason known only to Her. Perhaps it was Her plan all along to permit you the time needed to get things started—which you have. What you perceive as a deviation is just a minor course adjustment. The Goddess saw fit in Her infinite wisdom to spare you so you could fulfill your destiny.”

His comment brought tears to her eyes as she thought of how vibrant and full of life Lin and Piper were and of the choice they made to save a world they had adopted. It was their selfless act, which plunged her world into a darkness that seemed impossible to crawl out of, but was the motivation needed to allow Progensha to rise from the ashes of a tragedy and move forward toward a brighter future.

She thought of all they had accomplished in a relatively short period of time. She swiped a cloth across her runny nose and said, “I was unable to see what the Goddess tried to show me until you opened my eyes to the possibilities. Thank you.”

“Do not thank me. I was but a single instrument in the symphony of the Goddess’s plan.”

“But your sound was key in fostering a harmonious melody.”

T’iang simply bowed his head and then said, “Take pride in what you have accomplished.”

“What *we* have accomplished.”

He acknowledged her statement with a nod before he said, “Until we speak again.”

The screen went dark.

Martina's heart was filled with a surging pride and an assured confidence that the future of Progensha was in competent hands. She believed Lin and Piper would be proud.

Lexicon

Age of Majority - the age when a person is recognized as a full adult.

Andorra - former Thouron soldier turned resistance fighter.

Caprine - Progenshan equivalent of a goat.

Central Command - the main military command of the Thourons.

Chariot - the Uderran term for a car.

Colossal Sea - a large ocean off the coast of the northern continent.

Communicators - any device used to electronically communicate.

Dark Woods - a thickly wooded area of the northern continent.

Dart Lizard - a Plains animal that shoots paralysis darts immobilizing its prey. Equivalent to a Terran reptile.

Der'von - a high-ranking member of the Uderran High Council and leader of the Selemite Clan.

Directorate - the name of the intelligence division of the Thouron military.

Discards - members of Thouron society who are discriminated against due to their mixed heritage. Used interchangeably with Rejects.

Drat - a Progenshan curse word that translates loosely to shit or fuck.

Ekwin - Progenshan equivalent of a horse.

Exodus - the mass departure of citizens of Uderra shortly after the destruction of the Great Plains.

Fertile Valley - the area of the Great Plains the *Michael P Anderson* crashed in. It eventually became known as the Land of No Return.

Goddess - the primary deity worshiped by native Progenshans.

Grassy Plains - one of the names used to refer to the Great Plains.

Great Beyond - term the Plains People and other Progenshans use to refer to space or the cosmos.

Hill People - the people who eventually became the Thourons.

Jaydeen - one of Martina's three granddaughters.

Kazi - a high-ranking member of the Second Chance Mountain Clan.

Inland Seas - bodies of water that are safe to sail and fish because no leviathans live in them.

Land of No Return - the land once known as the Fertile Valley now contaminated by radiation and inhabited by mutated lifeforms.

Leviathan - monstrous sea creatures that roam/rule the oceans.

Lolaan - a high-ranking member of the Uderran High Council and leader of the Felid Clan.

Mar'jan - Martina's daughter.

Mectar - measure of distance equivalent to miles.

Memphis Lin - mother to Zuri and wife to Nicholas Piper.

Michael P Anderson - the name of the starship from the future that crashed in the Fertile Valley.

Micton - measure of time equivalent to minutes.

Mona - one of Martina's three granddaughters.

Mos - measure of time equivalent to one hour.

Mountain of the Goddess - the name the Uderrans call the largest mountain on the continent.

Mountainers - another term used to refer to the inhabitants of the Mountain of the Goddess or Second Chance Mountain.

Mud Boar - a forest animal that gores its prey.

Munchkin - nickname given to Zuri by her parents.

Nadir - an intelligence officer in the Thouron military.

Naron - an officer in the Thouron military and friend to Naron and Andorra.

Neander Thouron - a charismatic leader of the Thourons who is the originator of the bigoted doctrine that is the basis of their culture.

Nicholas Piper - father to Zuri and husband to Memphis Lin.

Open Valley - also referred to as the valley, glen, vale. Settled by the survivors of the crash who eventually became the founders of Traveler City.

Operation Save Progensha's Future - is the name given to the collective effort to rebuild the planet's future by Martina.

Passers - the name given to those of mixed heritage who look like Thourons.

Plains People - inhabitants of the Grassy Plains who became the Uderrans.

Progensha - the planet on which everything happens. It has two suns, and a pinkish-orange sky with white clouds.

Pyperlyn - the daughter of Zuri and T'yree.

Rejects - members of Thouron society who are discriminated against due to their mixed heritage. Used interchangeably with Discards.

Reunification - the term given to the effort to unify the descendants of those who survived the crash.

Second Chance Mountain - the name given to the Mountain of the Goddess by the survivors of the crash of the *Michael P Anderson* who lived there and their descendants.

Secton - measure of time equivalent to a second.

Shagnot - Progenshan equivalent to sheep.

She'ara - the queen of Uderra.

Siren - leader of the Dark Woods Clan.

Stuffie - a Progenshan word for a stuffed toy.

Sylvia - Martina's youngest granddaughter.

Talia - personal assistant to Der'von.

Tameen - personal assistant to Lolaan.

Thicket Tea - a medicinal herbal tea with hallucinogenic properties.

Thourons - Inhabitants of the planet Progensha. They live primarily in the hilly or rocky regions of the planet's largest continent.

T'iang - brother to Queen She'ara and father to T'yree.

Torchlight - a flashlight.

Traveler City Cultural Exchange and Engagement Center - the main hub in Traveler City used to connect the various ethnic groups.

Triquadi - a breed of Progenshan dog.

T'yree - husband to Zuri, father to Pyperlyn, and son of T'iang.

UCE - Uderran Corps of Engineers.

Uderra - the city-state founded by Memphis Lin and Nicholas Piper.

Uderrans - inhabitants of the city-state of Uderra. They are distantly related to the Thourons, but prefer to live in fertile valleys or grassy plains.

Virago - a highly irritating female; a wench.

Western Sea - one of the inland seas.

Wooders - term inhabitants of the Dark Woods use to refer to themselves.

Wraith - assistant to Siren.

Zuri - wife to T'yree, mother to Pyperlyn, and daughter of Memphis Lin and Nicholas Piper.

About the Author

Michael D. Brooks is a late bloomer baby boomer/joneser Indie Writer. He is a dreamer, fan of science fiction, enjoys humor, and is a kid at heart. He earned an MA in Writing Studies and has written numerous articles, Short Stories, Drabbles, and Flash Fiction.

The Destined series, an intricately woven tale of adventure, love, friendship, sacrifice, survival, and discovery has been noted to be on par with *Star Wars*, *Star Trek*, and *Dune*.

He is also the author of a humorous series of flash fiction books featuring conversations with a crusty but lovable character called Pop whose interactions and snippets of wisdom he imparts to his son and grandson often end with hilarious and insightful results.

Other Books by the Author

Conversations with Pop

More Conversations with Pop

Even More Conversations with Pop

Destined: by choice or circumstance

Intersections in Time

Beyond the Great Beyond

When Destinies Collide: every saga has a beginning

www.ingramcontent.com/pod-product-compliance
Lightning Source LLC
LaVergne TN
LVHW081251100826
845148LV00009B/1192

* 9 7 9 8 9 8 7 7 4 4 8 4 0 *